I0735755

Forbidden but Yours

....

Piper Westwood

Copyright © 2025 by Piper Westwood

All rights reserved.

No portion of this book may be reproduced in any form without written permission from the publisher or author, except as permitted by U.S. copyright law.

Contents

Chapter 1

I 've been best friends with Aubrey since I was four. We went to the same preschool and I ended up slapping her with a piece of turkey. Normally it would have gone on a sandwich but I wasn't into bread at the time. But I did it because she took my place mat with whinnie the Pooh on it. Some how after that little incident we became best friends during snack time. We shared some pretzels because my snack was obviously gone when I slapped her with it and she was nice enough to share hers.

Aubrey was the nicest person you could meet unless you pissed her off to the extreme. Like her brother does. Her brother is two years older than us. Or almost two years older. He's been away at military school because he got into a bunch of trouble. Not with just one thing but a lot of things. He hasn't been around since he was sixteen himself.

It's been a month since the school year started. Aubrey and I were sitting in her living room. She was laying on the floor with her legs on the couch with her phone above her scrolling through Facebook. My head was on her stomach and my right leg was on the couch doing the exact same thing she was. "Did you hear Lynn's pregnant?" She said. "Yeah that stupid hoe" I replied."Who's a hoe?" Someone asked coming in. I look up from my phone to see Jaxon. Aubrey's brother. He was in army pants and a dark blue t-shirt that showed off his muscles. He dropped a green duffel bag on the floor. "You are" Aubrey said laughing. He moved over me and pulled her away. My head hit the floor and I immediately sat up. I looked at them and laughed. They were play fighting like they use to when we were younger. "Okay I give"

Aubrey shouts. Jaxon gets off of her and looks at me. "Well you've changed" he said. "I hit puberty" I replied standing up and sitting down on the couch. "Makes sense since the last time I saw you I think you were what fourteen?" He replied. I nodded looking at my phone. I wasn't going to lie. Jaxon got hotter. If that's possible. Aubrey got up and grabbed her phone. She sat down next to me. "Why are you here?" She asked. I looked up at him. "Mom and dad didn't tell you? I'm back. For my senior year" he said sitting down on the chair. "Gonna do anything crazy?" She asked. "Nah I'm about to be an adult and can be charged as an adult if I get into anymore trouble. Plus military school kind of gets you out of that stuff" he answered. "I still can't believe you peed on a cop car" I said shaking my head. "I had to take a leak and I was drunk so" he replied shrugging his shoulders. I shook my head again and got up. I went to the kitchen and grabbed a Pepsi. I came back to the living room. "Your parents let you drink that now?" He asked with a smirk. "Shut up" I said sitting down and taking a drink.

My parents are a touchy subject to me. They got divorced a few months ago and don't really pay much attention to me. "I'm going to go unpack. Talk later" he said getting up and grabbing his bag. He looked at me and winked with a big ass smile on his face before he went upstairs.

Aubrey's parents gave us money for dinner because they were going to their annual company party for more investors . "Wanna go out to eat or order in?" She asked me. "Out" I answered wanting to go do something other than our usual which was sitting on the couch watching tv and being on our phones. She nodded. Jaxon came into the living room sitting down on the other couch. "We are going out for food. You wanna come?" Aubrey asks. He looks at us and smiles. "Yeah" he answered. He got up grabbed his keys from his front pocket of his joggers. I got off the couch and went to grab my bag which had my wallet in it. Aubrey already went out to the car and Jaxon stood by the door waiting for me so he could probably lock the door.

"Hey are we good?" He asked me.

"Yeah why wouldn't we be?" I asked.

"Because of my last night here" He answered. I tried not thinking about it. I didn't want to. I wanted to forget everything that happened the months leading up to it.

"We're fine let's get food. I'm hungry" I lied. He nodded his head looking down and we went to the car. I got in the back and so did Aubrey. "You know one of you can sit up front with me" he said after we got into the car because we were both sitting in the back of the car. Aubrey shrugged and looked at me. "Go" she said nudging me to go up front. I nodded and got out groaning to myself at having to sit next to him right now. I went up front and put my seat belt on. I took my phone from my pocket and looked at Facebook putting my attention to something else other than him. Jaxon took my phone out of my hands and put it in his pocket quickly. "Yo give it back" I said. "When we get back to the house" he replied with a smirk. "What about Aubrey's?" I complained. He shrugged and started driving.

I shook my head and crossed my arms leaning back into the seat.

We got to the Chinese restaurant and we got seated at a booth. I sat down by Aubrey and Jaxon was across from us. She took our drink orders and we went to get some food. After we sat back down and started eating some guys from school showed up. They were Jaxons old friends. He stood up and went over there to talk to them. "I hope he doesn't get involved with them again. They are part of the reason he got sent away" Aubrey said. I nodded looking over there. Jaxon looked over and winked at me. I shook my head and continued eating. I kept glancing over there at him.

Chapter 2

"Are you staying the night?" Aubrey asked as we were leaving the restaurant. "Yeah" I answered. She nodded and we got back into the car. This time she sat up front and I sat in the back looking out the window. I looked up front and caught him looking back at me from the little mirror. Jaxon drove us back to the house and we got out. Aubrey and I walked ahead of Jaxon and I looked back at him. He was staring at my butt. I shook my head and looked forward again. We went inside the house and went right up to her room. I laid down on her bed and she laid down next to me. "Wonder what schools going to be like tomorrow with Jaxon there" she said.

"Probably the same. Every girl wanting to be with him. Every guy will want to his friend again" I replied.

"Yeah that was always disgusting seeing girls hang on him most the time in the hallway. Or seeing the cheerleaders sitting on his lap in the lunchroom but then again it wasn't like that a few months before he went away. So it could be different" She responded.

"Doubt it" I said. I looked over at her and she was already falling asleep. I looked at the ceiling and took a deep breath closing my eyes as I let it out.

I woke up later that night having to go to the bathroom and of course I was thirsty. After going to the bathroom I went downstairs. I opened the fridge and grabbed a water bottle. I closed the door and turned around. I got pressed against the fridge and felt his mouth against mine. He pulled away and was smiling. He backed up smiling at me and then he turned around going upstairs. I shook my head wondering if I just imagined that. I walked back up the stairs and went back into Aubrey's room. I sat down on the bed and shook my head again. I took a drink of my water and put it on the night stand by her bed. I laid down trying to go back to sleep.

They next morning I used Aubrey's clothes. She has the same waist size as me but the chest. Not so much it fit but it was very snug. I came downstairs and Jaxson was looking at me. Aubrey was finishing her breakfast. "Ready to go?" She asked. I nodded. I looked at Jaxon one more time. He winked at me. Aubrey grabbed my hand and pulled me out of the house. We walked down the sidewalk. The school was only a few blocks away. I pulled my phone out checking it. No messages or calls from the parents. Again. Third night in a row not coming home you'd think they'd call but nope. Don't know why I even bother checking it for them. I put my phone in the back pocket of the skinny jeans I was wearing.

We were hanging out by our lockers and the doors opened. Everyone looked. It was Jaxon.

Girls mouths dropped. He was wearing a well fitted black shirt that showed off his muscles. Along with some dark blue jeans. He had his combat boots on too. I bit my lip and looked away. Okay it's true. I liked Jaxon and honestly we had a little secret. Aubrey would kill me if she found out about it. Before Jaxon left he kissed me. In the living room of his house before getting in the car and that wasn't all of it. We were kind of secretly dating behind her back. I knew if she found out we wouldn't be friends anymore. When I looked back he was smiling at me. He walked over and looked at Aubrey. "So the person who is suppose to show me my classes is our girl Lena" he said looking at me. I shrugged. I closed my locker. "The president of the student council always shows the new people around" I said. I started walking away. "You coming with or no?" I asked. He nodded and we walked to the office. "When did you get on the council?" He asked. "The last month before school ended. We did this election and surprisingly I won it. Didn't think I would've but here we are" I answered. We got his papers and walked out of the office. He put his hand on my waist stopping me and I looked at him."Are you going to pretend like last night didn't happen?" He asked. I looked at the ground."I think it's for the best. I don't want to hurt her" I answered. He tucked a piece of my hair behind my ear. "Aubrey doesn't have to know" he replied. I looked at him. "I can't lie to her again" I responded. "Lena" He said. I moved from him. "Your first class is right there" I said turning and walking away.

After school I walked to my house. I came in and my mom was sitting on a stool at the counter. She had her glasses on and on her work computer like she does everyday after she gets home. "Lena?" She asked. I walked into the kitchen. "Yeah mom" I said. "How was school?" She asked still looking at her computer. "Fine" I answered. She nodded. I turned around and went upstairs. I turned my radio on and went to my closet. I grabbed some shorts and a tank top. I went into the bathroom and got into the shower.

I walked out of the bathroom and Jaxon was on my bed. "What are you doing here?" I asked. He stood up and walked over to me. He grabbed my face gently and kissed me. I kissed him back and then pushed him away. He pulled me back into a kiss. He started walking backwards. He sat down and pulled me onto his lap. He moved down to my neck. "Jaxon" I said pushing him away. He put his forehead against my chest. "Lena I need you" he replied moving to look at me. "Things changed since you left" I responded. "Please" he begged. I took a deep breath. "I'm going to hell for this" I said. I pulled him into a kiss.

Chapter 3

"But what about the dance?" Someone asked. I was in the middle of a student council meeting and barely paying attention. Jaxon was on my mind. Aubrey was on my mind. Before Jaxon left we started something. We weren't exactly dating because of Aubrey but we had a few kisses here and there. Spent time together. I was there when he got busted for peeing on a cop car. Aubrey didn't know I was there. She just thought I was walking by. I was in love with him. Have been since I got to know him. Then he left for military school. I didn't hear from him. He just vanished. He called every week for his parents and of course Aubrey. But I didn't get one. Thought he changed his mind about me. All these thoughts were going through my head. I know I said earlier that we were kind of dating and that was wrong. He never asked me to be his girlfriend or anything but it felt like we were because we were together almost every night. I remember sneaking out after my parents went to bed because I wanted to see him and he wanted to see me.

"Lena" someone said snapping back to reality. "Yes?" I asked. "I think we should have a mystery ball for the dance. What do you think?" The girl asked. "I like it" I answered. She nodded and wrote it down. "That's the end of the weekly meeting" our advisor said. I got up and grabbed my bag. I walked out of the door and Aubrey was waiting outside on her phone. "Jaxon tried out for football. He just got done so he can take us to the mall" she said. I nodded. We went out to the football field and waited for him to come out. Aubrey was so focused on her phone she didn't see him come up. He walked behind her and went behind me. He lightly smacked my butt and smiled. I shook my head looking at Audrey who had all of her attention on her phone. "Ready to go?" He asked making Aubrey jump. "Yeah let's go" she answered. "So why are we going shopping?" He asked. "Lena found out the theme of the dance so we are going shopping before anyone else clears out the good stuff" Aubrey answered. "The dance?" He replied. "It's next weekend if you wanna ask anyone" she responded. "Good to know" he said looking at me.

Both of us found some dresses and went into the changing rooms. I had on a long black dress. I was looking at myself in the mirror. The door opened and I saw Jaxon in the mirror. I turned around. "If Aubrey sees you..." I started. "Relax. She's in the dressing rooms on the other end because someone else is in the one next to you" he interrupted me whispering. He grabbed my waist and pulled me to him. I put my hands on his chest. He bent his head down and kissed me. I moved my hands wrapping them around his neck and kissed him back. He bent down and put his hands on the back of my thighs. He lifted me up and pressed me against the wall. He moved down to my neck. I tugged on his hair and he groaned. He pulled back and smiled. "Wanna be my date?" He asked. "I don't know" I answered. "Everyone will be wearing mask. She won't even know if you don't let her see which one you have on" he replied. I bit my lip and he looked at me doing it. "Let me think about it" I finally answered. He smiled. He put me down and stood back to look at me. "That dress doesn't do you justice" he said. He walked right out.

I went back to my house after we went shopping. I went upstairs and put my dress in the closet. I came out to turn some music on and Jaxon was sitting on my bed again. "We are going out" he said. "Umm what?" I replied. He got off of the bed and went into my closet. He came out with a hoodie and grabbed my hand. He pulled me to the window and I stopped him. "We can go out the front door" I said. "Then your parents will know" he replied. "No they won't. Trust me" I responded walking to the door with him following me. We went downstairs. My mom was again in the kitchen working on her computer. We walked right out the door without her noticing. "That was weird" he said when we got into the car. "Not really" I replied. "What do you mean?" He asked. "They got divorced. Moms mostly on the computer doing work when she's home" I answered. "When did that happen?" He asked. "Few months ago" I answered. He nodded and drove off not asking about it anymore.

Jaxon took me to one of his spots. We got out and there were his old friends partying around a bonfire. He took my hand and led me out there. "Thought you weren't going to get into anymore trouble" I said. "It's just a fire" he replied. I nodded and rolled my eyes. It was never just a fire. Onetime someone got pushed into that fire because everyone was drinking too much or high or even both. We got some drinks and he sat down on one of the chairs pulling me down on his lap. "Jaxon my man" Miles said smiling. Jaxon nodded his head in his direction. "Still banging the same chick huh?" He said smiling at me. "Always"

Jaxon said smiling. "Lena lovely as ever" Nelson said holding his cup out to me. Jaxon laughed. "Still suck at those moves man" he said. They all laughed. I snuggled back into Jaxon. Everyone got into their own conversations. "Can I ask you something?" I said. "Of course" he said taking a drink. "Why didn't you contact me at all when you were away?" I asked. "I didn't want you to be mad at me. Or think different of me. You were there that night. And I packed my bags the next morning. I tried to get over you so you could do better than me. I dated some girls there but none of them compared to you. I didn't know how to tell you anything" he answered. I sat up from him. "So while I was here. Not seeing anyone. Keeping it a secret that we were messing around you were messing around with other girls?" I said. "Lena it's not like that" he replied. I shook my head and got up from his lap. I walked off. He followed me of course. "Lena come on. Please. I didn't think I was going to see you for a long time. When I did. I felt this ping in my chest and you played it off easily. That I was nothing more to you than Aubrey's older brother. Not the first guy you've ever kissed. Or gave the one special part of you away that you could never get back" he said. "I gave that to you the night you got in trouble" I replied. "Yeah. And I bet my sister still has no idea that you aren't a virgin" he responded. I looked away from him. "I was stupid and young" I said. "So you regret it?" He asked. I looked him in the eyes. "I was too young and I fell for you. I thought we would be together for real after but you got busted right after. I felt like you planned it when you didn't talk to me" I answered. "I didn't plan it. I was drunk. We went out to a party after. Then I did something stupid" he replied. I shook my head. He walked over to me. "I didn't plan anything. I was a dumb sixteen year old. I did things that I shouldn't have done. I know I shouldn't have done that stuff with you that night. That I should've waited a little longer. I shouldn't have answered the phone after. That we should've stayed in our secret spot" he said. He pushed my hair behind my ear. "I love you Lena. Nothing has ever changed that" he added. "I love you" I said. He smiled. "You have no idea how much I've missed you saying that" he replied. "I only said it to you once before" I responded. He smiled. "Still missed it" he said. He pulled me into a kiss.

Chapter 4

I woke up to my phone alarm going off. I was laying on my side and reached for my phone. I turned it off and laid back down. I felt kisses on my shoulder. I looked back and smiled. He smiled at me. "Morning" He said."Morning" I replied turning to face him. "We have to get ready for school" he said. I nodded. He kissed me and got out of the bed. I tried not laughing again at his boxers. "Stop" He said looking at me. I looked away. "I mean what seventeen year old has that on his boxers?" I replied getting out of the bed. "What sixteen year old still wears mini mouse on her panties and bras?" He responded.

"You have scooby doo on yours" I defended. He shrugged. He pulled on his jeans and tossed me his shirt. I grabbed it and put it on over my tank top. I took my shorts off and pulled on some skinny jeans. I tucked his white v neck shirt into the jeans and pulled my hair into a pony tail. He grabbed a shirt from the closet and I went to the window. I grabbed the tree branch and climbed down like I use to do. I walked to the front door and rung the door bell. Aubrey answered the door and I walked in looking at Facebook on my phone. Jaxon came down and sat down at the table eating Aubrey's eggs. "Hey mom made you some before she left. Why do you have to eat mine?" She asked. He shrugged and winked at me. I shook my head. "Mom made some for you too" she said grabbing a plate with some more eggs. I grabbed the other plate that had some on them too.

We got to school and Aubrey ran off because she had to talk to her math teacher about extra credit to get her grade up. I went to my locker and he leaned against the ones next to mine. "What do you want to do tonight?" He asked. "Aubrey and I have movie night on fridays" I answered. He nodded. "Maybe I'll join" he said. "Or maybe you can stay the night Saturday" I replied. "Oh I get it. Need some girl time. But yeah I can do that. I'll be the one coming through the window" he said smiling and walked away. I shook my head and went to my first class.

After school Aubrey and I took over the living room. We did our homework for two hours. Math can take awhile to solve the problems. Jaxon headed out the door in the middle of saying he will be back later. "He found a new hoe" Aubrey said. "What do you mean?" I asked. "He's been talking to Marsha at school. Last night he went out and didn't come back until late. I heard him sneak a girl inside. I didn't look out my door because I didn't know what he was doing with her to know if it was Marsha" she answered. I nodded and looked back at the book biting my lip. When we got our homework done we ordered in. I ordered from Grubhub. I changed into shorts and a tank top. I put on my little slipper boots and went into the living room. Aubrey was chang-ing too. I turned Netflix on and put after on. I paused it until Aubrey got back and sat down on the couch. Just as she sat down my phone went off. I answered it. Our food was here. I got up. I grabbed the five for the tip and went outside. The delivery guy got out of the car and looked at me holding the bag. "Well aren't you something" he said. He was older and a little creepy. "I'm sorry?" I replied. "Oh baby don't play dumb" he responded. "Can I just have our food?" I said. "I have a little dinner for you" he replied. I too a step back and he dropped our bag on the ground. He grabbed me and pushed me to the ground. I screamed and started fighting him off but he restrained my hands above my head. He slapped me hard and used one hand to grab my jaw. "Scream and I'll make it hurt" he said. A gun went off. He looked up. I did too. It was Aubrey holding her dads 42 to the air. She pointed it at him. "Get the fuck off of her" she yelled. He got off of me and ran to his car. He got in and sped off. I sat up crying and she rushed over to me. She held me for a few minutes until Jaxon pulled into the drive way. Within those minutes it started to sprinkle and we were wet. "What happened?" He asked looking at me. "You're bleeding" he said touching my face. I flinched before his hand touched my cheek. "Call the cops" Aubrey said. He looked at us and nodded. He got up and walked a few feet away taking his phone out of his pocket.

Chapter 5

I didn't sleep much that night. The fact that someone would do that. To a female upset me. Before I went to bed I made sure everything was locked. Windows and doors. When it came to five in the morning I got out of Aubrey's bed and went to the door. I unlocked it and went outside. Jaxon was sitting on a chair outside the room with a baseball bat. He looked like he didn't get any sleep either. He looked at me. "Hey you okay?" He asked standing up. I nodded. He pulled me into a hug. I hugged him back. "Let's go downstairs" he said pulling away. We went downstairs. Alison his mom was making coffee. She looked up at us. "Hey kiddos" she said. "Are you doing any better?" She asked. I shrugged. "I see you guys got no sleep" she said. "I was worried about her so I stayed up with a base ball bat outside Aubrey's room" Jaxon said. She nodded. "Luckily your dad had his gun here" she said. He nodded. I sat down at the table. Alison didn't say much after that. She just got her morning coffee and made some breakfast for us. I didn't touch it. I wasn't feeling hungry. Jaxon pulled me to him. I rested my head on his shoulder. I closed my eyes and felt very tired. I felt him pick me up and carry me upstairs. I gripped his shirt the whole way up there. I felt the bed beneath me and I let his shirt go.

I woke up later on. I was in Jaxons room. He was sleeping on the floor. Aubrey walked in and sat down by me. "Are you feeling okay?" She asked. "Yeah. I'm tired" I answered. She nodded. "Jaxon told me you didn't sleep. That you went downstairs and fell asleep at the kitchen table so he brought you in here. He didn't want to wake me up. I'm okay with it. I just hope that you're okay after last night" she replied. "I don't think I'm ever getting Grubhub again" I responded. "Never again" she said agreeing with me."Why don't you get some more sleep and Jaxon will take you home if you want" she added."I think I'm gonna walk home. Do you mind if I take the bat with me?" I replied. She nodded. I got out of the bed. I went into her room and changed into different clothes. I grabbed my bag. On the way out of her room I grabbed the bat that was against the wall.

Later on when I was home I was laying in my bed when Jaxon came through the window. He came over to the bed and took his shoes off. He got into the bed and pulled me close to him. "I could have brought you home" he said. "You needed sleep" I replied. "I could sleep here. With you" he responded. "You're here now. So let's just cuddle" I said. He smiled and pulled me closer to him. He put my leg over his. I snuggled my head closer to his chest. I ran downstairs to the kitchen. Jaxon was following me downstairs. He grabbed my waist and pulled me to him. "I'm hungry" I said smiling. "Let's go out" he replied.

"It's late. What place is open at 11" I responded. "I know a few places" he said. I nodded. He grabbed my hand and pulled me out the door. He took me to sheetz. We went to the order computer. He stood behind me with his hand on my waist. We ordered food. He went to pay and I stayed near the food. He came back and smiled at me. "See I know a few places that are open" he said smiling at me. "Yeah I forgot about sheetz. We came here a lot" I replied. "After every hang out I brought you here. We would eat. Talk and then I'd take you home" he responded. I smiled. "186" the lady called. We went over there and grabbed our food. We went out to the sitting area outside. He kissed the side of my forehead and we started eating. We got back to my house. I grabbed two waters and we went upstairs. I turned the tv onto Netflix and put on Hart of Dixie. I laid back on my bed and he did the same thing.

"Didn't we watch this awhile ago?" He asked.

"Yes but it's my favorite show" I answered.

"I only remember that because of the way you reacted to the ending. You started kicking your feet shrieking because you loved the way it ended" He replied.

"Yeah because it was amazing" I responded.

"It's a sappy ending" He said. My mouth dropped.

"Shut up" I replied. He laughed.

"How many times have you watched this show though?" He asked.

"Hmm don't know. A lot" I answered. He shook his head.

"Did you watch anything else?" he replied.

"Yes I did. You're forgetting I'm the binge queen" I responded.

"My queen" He said. I looked at him with a smile.

"And my king" I replied.

Chapter 6

Aubrey and I were playing Mario cart in the game room. "No" she yelled. Someone knocked her out of first place with the red shell making me be the one in first place. I laughed and crossed the finish line. "Ridged. The game is ridged" she said. "Bree it's just a game" I replied. "You're only saying that because you won" she responded shaking her head and leaning back against the couch. "Even if I didn't it's still just a game" I said putting the controller down and leaned back."I've always sucked at that game" she said glaring at me. "Sucked? Dude you've won almost all of those rounds" I replied. She shrugged. I shook my head and crossed my arms. "Wanna order in?" She asked. I glared at her. "I'll make sure Jaxon gets it before he leaves" she added. I nodded. She went to get the Chinese menu from the fridge and came back with the phone too. "Order my usual. I have to pee" I said getting up. She nodded putting the phone to her ear. I walked down the hall and opened Jaxons door. I walked inside and sat down on his bed. He came out of his bathroom in a towel that hung low on his hips. "Hey what are you doing in here?" He asked coming closer to me. "Aubrey's ordering food and you have to get it when they come here before you leave" I answered. He nodded. "That's fine. I don't mind doing that" he said. "Where are you going?" I asked. "To a party" he answered. I nodded. "I'd ask if you would like to come but you're hanging with Bree" he said. "As long as you crawl into my bed at night it's fine" I replied standing up. I went to the door and he gently grabbed my arm. I turned towards him. "Your bed is the only bed I want to be in" he responded. "Good" I said. I kissed his cheek and left his room. I went to the bathroom like I said I was going to.

Bree was passed out on the little couch and I was half way asleep on the big couch when the door opened. I looked up and saw Jaxon stumbling in the house. He was being supported by two guys because he couldn't walk by himself. Bree woke up to this too. I went over to them. "I got him" I said. I grabbed his arm and put it around my shoulder. Bree went to his other and did the same. "One of us has to escort them out" I said to her. She nodded and followed behind the guys as they made their way out. I got Jaxon upstairs to his room and helped him into his bed. I took his shoes off and tosses them towards his closet. I pulled his jeans down and tossed those too. I grabbed one of his blankets and covered him up with one. Bree came up as I got done. "Mom and dad are going to be pissed to see this side of his again" she said crossing her arms. "Bree it was just one party and he's home. He didn't do anything bad that we know of" I replied. "Why are you defending him?" She asked. "Because. He just got back. Do you think he would be that stupid to risk getting sent back? Or worse. Jail?" I answered. "I guess you're right" she responded. "I do know. If he pukes on me again I'm punching him in his balls this time" I replied walking away. "I remember that night" she said laughing and shaking her head. "Shut up and let's go to bed. I'm exhausted" I replied walking into her room. I got under her blanket and she did the same. "Night" I said. "Good night" she replied.

The next morning Jaxon came down holding his head. Bree got up and dumped his shoulder walking out the door. "Is she on her period or something?" He groaned. I shook my head and did the same thing as her but harder. He stumbled into the wall. He groaned even louder. "Babe what the hell?" He asked. "Yeah. Exactly. What the hell Jax. You came home drunk. Very drunk" I snapped at him. "Please don't yell" he whined a little. I shook my head and followed Bree out of the house. I ran to catch up with her. "Bet he's not coming to school" she said shaking her head.

"I wouldn't make that bet" I replied looking back and saw him coming out of the house wearing a hoodie and sunglasses following behind us.

Chapter 7

walked home after school. I didn't want to deal with Jaxon or Bree. All she did was complain about him all day to all of us in our friend group and I was tired of it. Jaxon tried to talk to me a lot about it but of course I ignored him. The silent treatment should do him some good honestly. I went downstairs and saw a note from my mom. There was two hundred dollars by it. She went away on a business trip for a few days. I grabbed the money and went to my room. I went to my closet and grabbed my box. I opened it and pulled out the bag of money that was in there. I put it in the box. Whenever my mom would leave

I saved the money. Or when my parents fought a lot they would both give me money. I had about ten thousand or more all together in there. I put the money back in the box and put the box back. I walked out of the closet and laid back against the bed.

I was snuggled up in my bed with Netflix on. I turned my phone off before I started watching anything because honestly Bree was getting too much about Jax and he also wouldn't stop blowing up my phone too. My window was locked and the curtains were closed. The house was also locked up good too. I wanted to be left alone for a little bit obviously. But that wasn't happening because some decided to break my window and climb in. And yes. That someone was Jaxon. "Why haven't you been answering me?" He asked panting. "I wanted to be alone" I answered. He looked around the room and then at me. He came over and ripped the blanket off of me. "Have you been taking your medications?" He replied. I glared at him. I felt angry. "Yes now get out" I yelled. He threw the blanket back down on me. "I only care about your well being" he yelled back. "My well being is fine. Fine enough where my doctor said I didn't need them anymore. Even with my parents divorce" I said. "What about your iron?" He asked. I looked at the tv not wanting to say anything else. "It's still bad isn't it?" He said. "I'm fine" I replied. He got in bed with me. "The last time you were like this you shut down completely. Bree came home with tears in her eyes scared. She was scared about what was happening to you" he responded. "I'm better now" I said. He nodded. "Sometimes I just like being alone. I'm always with Aubrey. Always anymore. Once in awhile I like to stay in bed. Watch movies and relax completely without having to talk. Also like wearing no pants or a bra" I added. He nodded. "Well we can do that together" he said. He stripped down to his boxer and pulled the blanket back to get underneath it. He looked at the tv and didn't say anything. "You're fixing my window right?" I asked. "Yes I'll fix it. But not right now" he answered. I shook my head glaring at him and looked at the tv.

Jaxon walked in with a new window and went right to my room. I went downstairs and made some hot pockets. I grabbed some plates and put one on each of them. I waited for him to get done. He came down and sat down next to me. He took a bite and looked at me. I took a bite of mine and he was still looking at me. "What?" I asked."Are you mad about the party?" He said. "I don't want you to get sent away again" I replied. "I'm not going to" he responded. "How do you know that? You came home really drunk Jax. If your parents saw that you would be on the way back to military school" I said. "Babe I'm not going anywhere I promise" he replied. I looked away from him. "Alright. How about this. When I party. I'll come here so they don't know" he said. I looked at him. "Fine" I replied. He smiled and pushed my hair behind my ear. "When I turn 18 I'll try to get my own place. So we won't have to worry about much" he responded. I nodded. He kissed my forehead and went back to eating.

"Tomorrow is Friday. I think just maybe we could go to the party with Jaxon instead of watching movies" Bree said later on when I went back to their house. "If he will let us go" I replied mostly meaning it about her. She shrugged. "I think he will let us" she responded. "Jaxon" she yelled. He came into her room and leaned against the door frame. "What's up?" He asked. "We want to go to the party with you tomorrow" she said. He looked at me then back at her. "Bree I get to have a say on your clothes. Do not and I mean do not put your drink down for a second. And do not take a drink from anyone. You go get it yourself. You have to go to the bathroom you take Lena with you. Don't go anywhere alone. If you see some friends okay. Just stay safe. I don't want to spend my night babysitting when I would love to have some fun with my own friends" he replied. "What about Lenas clothes? Or telling her this stuff?" She asked. "Lena is right there and she can wear whatever she wants because she's not my little sister. I'll protect her if I need to. Just like I would you. But like I said. She's not my sister to say that stuff to" he answered. She nodded. He looked at me. "But I would prefer if you didn't wear clothes that revealed to much" He added. I glared at him and he smirked at me. I rolled my eyes.

Chapter 8

"Oh come on Jaxon" Bree whined. "No" he said. She stomped back upstairs to change her clothes again. He came over to me. He grabbed my tights. "Hey you're gonna put a hole in these" I said. "I like these on you" he said. He started to kiss my neck and I closed my eyes. "How come Lena can wear shorts?" Bree yelled down the stairs. He pulled away and walked to the steps. "She has tights on underneath them. And she has a button up flannel with a tank top on. You just had shorts and a tank" he said. She groaned and went back upstairs. He laughed looking at me. He came back over to me and pulled me against his body. "Maybe I can take you home with me tonight" He joked. I laughed and pushed him away. I walked to the steps and looked at him. "Or I'll be the one bringing you home" I said. I went upstairs to Aubrey's room and she was sitting on the floor in her bra and underwear. She looked at me. "Help me please" she said. I nodded and went over to her closet. I pulled out some dark skinny jeans. I tossed them at her. I grabbed on of her jean button up vest. I came out. She was wearing the jeans. I went over to her dresser and grabbed a black bra to match the vest. I went over to her. "Put this on. Then the vest don't put anything on under the vest. Its going to show your belly button but it's fine" I said. I walked out and downstairs. "I dressed her. Don't send her back up" I said. He nodded. She came down and he shook his head and looked at me. "She's hot and not revealing too much" I said. "Fine lets go" He replied. He walked out of the house and we followed him. "What did you say to get him okay with this?" She asked. I smiled.

We got to the party. Jaxon walked in ahead of us and when we got in Bree instantly went to her other friends leaving me alone. I went to the kitchen and saw Jaxon leaning against the counter with a drink in his hand already. I went over to him and grabbed his drink. He smiled at me when I took a drink. I gave it back to him. "Where's Bree?" He asked. "With some friends" I answered. He nodded. He grabbed my hand and led me through a hallway. He opened up a door and pulled me inside. It was a bedroom. I looked at him and pulled his head down to kiss him. I was buttoning up my shirt and I looked at him. He smiled at me."Sorry. I couldn't wait to get you out of those tights" he said. I laughed and shook my head. He came over to me and moved my hands away. He started buttoning the last two for me while looking in my eyes. I bit my lip and he stopped buttoning it up. "We should probably get back out there before she notices we are gone" he said. "Yeah" I replied. He took a step back and went out of the door. I followed a minute later and he was back in the kitchen getting a drink. I went out to the living room and saw Bree dancing with the girls. I smiled at her when she looked up at me. I went to get two drinks and I went out to them. I gave her a drink and started dancing. "You have a hickey" she said. I froze. "You might want to cover it up before we go home. Jaxon might not want to say anything but he's protective over you too" she added. I nodded. We started dancing again and having some fun.

"Jaxon can you even take us home?" Bree asked. Jaxon was drunk. Again. "Here. Take my keys and I'll call an Uber when I'm leaving" he said handing me the car keys. I took them and we left. I pulled in front of her house. "I'm just dropping you off. I'm gonna head home" I said getting out of the car too. "Take Jaxsons car. I bet he'll find it tomorrow when he's sober" she replied. I nodded and got back into the car. I drove home and pulled into my drive way. Moms car still wasn't here. I got out and went inside. I went upstairs and sat down on my bed. My phone went off and I answered it. "Babe unlock

the door" he said. I laughed and went downstairs.
I unlocked the door and opened it. He came in
pulling me to him. He pulled me into a kiss and
backed me up against the wall. He kicked the
door closed. He bent down and lifted me up. He
carried me up the stairs and into my room. He
set me down on the bed and took his shoes off.
He got on top of me and kissed me again.

Chapter 9

I woke up seeing Bree standing in my room. She dropped everything she was carrying. I got out of bed and realized what she saw. Jaxon. Me in his shirt. Shit. "Bree I can explain" I said. She started running out of the room and I followed her. "Bree please" I said. "He's going to use you. He got what he wanted. And you betrayed the trust I had. That's my brother. You had sex with my brother. How long? How long was that going on behind my back?" She demanded turning back to look at me. "Two and a half years" I said. She slapped me. She slapped me hard enough to cause my mouth to bleed. "We are done. I don't want to see you around anymore. Our friendship is over and has been nothing but a lie. You're gonna get your heart broken. Don't come crying to me when it happens" she replied running down the street. I started to cry. I went back inside the house and into my room. I took his shirt off and grabbed his jeans. I went over to him and pushed him out of my bed. He landed with a thump. "What the hell?" He said. "Get out" I said. "What?" He asked. "Get the fuck out" I answered pushing him to the door. "Babe what's wrong" he said. "Don't call me that anymore. Don't call me. Don't come over. Just get out" I yelled. I slammed my bed room door in his face and leaned my back against it. I started to cry harder. I fell to the ground and hugged my knees to my chest.

I turned my phone off. I didn't want to hear from anyone. I went downstairs and locked the door. I made sure all doors and windows were locked. I went to the kitchen and opened the fridge door. Nothing popped out at me to eat or drink. I closed the door and went to my room. I turned the tv on and laid in bed. It wasn't long before I heard knocking on the door. I ignored it. A minute passed and someone was trying to come in through the window. I ignored it. I didn't want to talk to Jaxon. I just wanted to stay in bed and ignore everything. I lost my best friend. I sat up when the glass shattered on my window. Jaxon came in. "Why do you do that? Can't you tell I don't want to be bothered?" I demanded. He grabbed the board that was over the last one he broke and put it over the window. He came over to me and pulled me out of the bed. He kissed me. I pushed him away. "I know what happened. Bree knows. She's pissed off. But who cares? This relationship is ours. She will get over it. Just give her some time" he said. "She doesn't want to be friends Jax" I replied. He pulled me into his arms. "She even hit me" I added. He pulled back a little bit and looked at my mouth. He shook his head. "Babe everything will be back to normal in a month. Trust me" he said. I took a deep breath. "At least we don't have to hide anymore" he added. I smiled. "Yeah but that part was fun" I replied. He laughed. "Not as fun as being able to take you to the dance this weekend and being able to dance with you and kiss you" he responded. I nodded. "Next time something bad happens. Please don't shut me out again. Or shove me out or even push me out of bed" he said. I laughed. "That shit hurt" he added. He took his shirt off and his shoes. He got into my bed and tossed his shirt at me. I took the hoodie I was wearing off and put his shirt on. I climbed into bed next to him and snuggled into him.

Another party. This time I could stay with Jaxon. I was wearing skinny jeans and his shirt tucked into them. He pulled me out into the woods. And yes it's the same spot as the first time we partied. We sat down on a log near the fire. Some guys passed and high fives Jax. I got up and went to get a drink. I stopped when I got closer. Bree was standing there with a guy. I went back to Jaxon and pulled him up. "What's going on?" He asked. I pulled him to where I was and pointed."Oh fuck no" he said. He went over there and pulled her aside. They started fighting and he lifted her over his shoulder and walked back to me. "Let's go" He said. I followed behind him and Bree was glaring at me. We got back to the house and she stormed inside. We followed behind her and the parents were in the living room with their arms crossed. "Where were you both?" Their dad asked. "A party" Bree answered crossing her arms. "Jaxon I thought we talked about this" their mom said. I looked at the ground. He grabbed my hand. "Lena and I both went to the party. We didn't drink. All we did was hang out with friends. Bree here was with random guys drinking. Go ahead and smell her breath" Jaxon said. Their dad walked up to Bree. "Open your mouth" he yelled when she refused. She rolled her eyes and did it. He went over to Jaxon and Jaxon did it without refusing. He came in front of me. I opened my mouth and breathed out. He stepped back. He looked at Bree. "You're grounded for two months. And no. Lena is not an exception" he said. "That's fine because we aren't friends anymore" she replied going upstairs. "What does that mean?" Her mom asked looking at me. Jaxon raised our hands in the air and they saw."How long?" She asked. "Two and a half years" Jaxon answered. "But that was way before you left" his dad said. Jaxon nodded. "And she just found out" his mom smiled. "Just like how we were" his dad replied. They laughed and walked away. I was left confused.

Chapter 10

"Mom fell for her brothers best friend which is my dad" Jax said. I nodded. We sat down on the couch and I laid my legs over his lap. He put his one arm on them and the other on the back of the couch behind me. "Was your uncle okay with it?" I asked. "Not at first" he answered. I nodded. "But with some time he got use to the idea of having his best friend be with his sister. That he was already family so" he added. "I'm already family?" I asked. "You've been best friends with Bree since you were what four or five?" He replied. I nodded. "You're also always here so I'd say yeah. You're apart of the family" he added. I snuggle into him and he moves his arm from the back of the couch around me. He kissed my forehead and rubs my side. His mom came in with a bag and put it on my legs. She leaves the room and Jaxon opens it. He laughs. "What?" I asked. "Rubbers" he answered. I start laughing too.

Jaxon took me back to my house. We went upstairs and it was colder in my room. I look at him. "I know. I know. I gotta fix it" he said. "Why don't we go back to my house tonight and tomorrow morning I'll come back and fix it?" He suggested. I nodded and grabbed my bag. I went over to the closet and grabbed some clothes. "You don't have to bring clothes babe" he said smiling. "Then what am I going to wear?" I asked. "My stuff" he answered. "I can't wear it to school Monday" I replied. "You can wear my sweats and a shirt" he shrugged. I nodded and left my bag. We went back to his house. Going upstairs we heard. "Don't forget protection" from his dad. "No grand babies yet" his mom called up too."Run" He said. I nodded and we ran up to his room. He closed the door and locked it shaking his head. I went over to his dresser and grabbed a shirt. I stripped out of my clothes and put it on. He pulled me to him. He was on the bed and laid back with me on top of him. He started to tickle me and I laughed. "Jax stop please" I begging in between laughs. He stopped and pulled me closer to him. "What do you want to do?" He asked. "I want food" I answered. He nodded and pulled his phone out. He ordered pizza. "Should be here in a half an hour" he said putting his phone away. I nodded and put black ops 3 in. He sat down next to me and grabbed a controller. "Ready to kick some zombie ass?" He asked. "Yes" I answered smiling. He nodded and we started the game. "Jaxon I need you to give me a ride" Bree said coming in his room without knocking. I look at her and she was on her phone. "You're grounded" he replied. She looked up only to glare at us. "You just don't want to stop playing you're stupid game with your hoe" she responded. I saw his hand tighten on the controller. He set it down and stood up. He was facing her. "Lena is not a hoe. Just because we are in a relationship does not mean you need to treat her this way. She's been your best friend for years. Stop being a baby and get over it" he yelled. She grabbed his book off the stand and threw it at him. He ducked and it hit my head and I fell off his bed. I got up and put my hand to the spot it hit. He came over to me and looked at it. "Aubrey get out" he yelled. She rolled her eyes and stormed out. "Still think she needs time?" I asked. "I don't know what's wrong with her" he answered. "She hates me" I replied. "I'll be right back. I'm gonna go get some ice for your head" he responded. I nodded and he left the room. I heard yelling from downstairs. It was their parents and Bree's voices. I heard Jaxon yell in a few times. A few minutes passed and he came upstairs with some ice. Aubrey's door slammed shut.

Chapter 11

Once it got around that I was dating a senior and not just any senior. But Jaxon. It was hell. Girls glared at me. Rumors started. I went over to Jaxon after school and a lot of people were looking at us. "Get over it people. They've been dating for two years if you haven't noticed before" Nelson shouted at everyone. "Thanks man" Jaxon said. "I wonder if she knows about Marsha" a girl said out loud while passing us. I look at Jaxon. "That I'm gonna have to explain" he said looking at me. "But not in the eyes and hears of the public" Nelson said. Jax nodded and put his hand on my waist leading me out of the schools parking lot.

"So Marsha" I said. "I met her a few months ago at the spring formal. Her brother goes to school there and he asked her to come because we could have our families visit. We started fooling around. A month went by and then two weeks. She came to see me. Said she was pregnant. Said it was mine. I called up my dad and talked to him. Asked him not to say anything to Aubrey because I knew it would get back to you and I didn't want to hurt you that way. But anyways. He said I had to see if it was mine. We went to do a DNA test. Turns out it wasn't mine. So when I first got here I saw her here in the same school as you. I talked to her. Asked her how she was doing. You know being nice. But it got around that we fooled around" he said. I nodded."People are saying she's pregnant with my baby" he added. "Okay so let them. It's obviously not yours" I said. He pulled me to him. I wrapped my arms around him and closed my eyes."I'm sorry for doing anything while I was in military school" he said. "It's fine" I replied. He tightened his arms around me.

I came out of the downstairs bathroom and pushed into a wall. Bree has her arm against my throat. "Marsha is pregnant with my little niece or nephew. Do not mess this up for my brother" she said. I wanted to roll my eyes. I pushed her away."It's not his" I replied. "That's not what she's saying" she responded. "Your brother got a DNA test" I said. "Yeah and it came back positive" she replied."No it didn't" I responded. "Yes it did" she said. I pushed her further away from me and went upstairs to his room. I slammed the door and he looked at me from his game. "What's wrong?" He asked. "Do you still have the papers from the DNA test?" I replied. "Yeah why?" He responded. "Can I see them?" I asked. He got up from the bed and went over to his army duffel bag and took them out. He walked over and gave them to me. I looked at them. "What's going on?" He asked. "Bree said the test came back positive" I answered. He shook his head. "She's just try-ing to break us up" he replied. It was negative."I don't understand why she's doing this to me" I responded. I sat down on his bed and put the papers down. He sat down next to me. "Everything is going to be okay. She'll come around eventually" he said.

Everyday at school I kept getting glares and talked about. Saying I was a home wrecker and a slut for being with Jaxon. Everyone was on Marsha's side. Everyone but Jaxon's friends. They were the only ones I hung with the whole week. Them and Jaxon. When the dance came up I didn't feel like going because of it. But Jaxon convinced me to go. I was currently looking in my body mirror at myself in the dress. It was a short sparkly black dress. It was a little puffed out. It didn't have any straps to it. My hair was half up and half down the part that was down was curled. I put on my black wedges. I grabbed my black mask. I put it on and went downstairs. Jaxon walked in through the door and stopped at me. "Wow" He said. "Where's your mask?" I asked. He pulled it out of the inside pocket of his tux. It was black to match me. I smiled. He pulled out a white and black flower. I smiled. He put it on my wrist and we went to his car. He opened the door for me and I got inside. He got in on the other side. I looked in the back and Bree was back there on her phone.

Chapter 12

When we got there a lot of people looked our way. I could see Marsha looking over here. I did notice her baby bump then. I looked away. I noticed no one was wearing their masks. I took mine off and walked to a table. Jaxon followed me. I sat down and set my mask on the table. He sat down next to me. He took his off and set it with mine. Miles and Nelson came over with their dates and sat down at the table. Jaxon put his arm around the back of my chair. "Want to dance?" Jaxon asked. I nodded. We got up from the table and he pulled me to the middle of the gym floor. I wrapped my arms around his neck and he wrapped his around my waist. He kissed my forehead. We danced for a few songs and then I got pulled away from Jaxon. I looked by who and it was by a few of Marsha's friends. "Who the hell do you think you are dancing with someone else's man?" She demanded. I saw Bree stop near and watch. "I'm dancing with my man" I said. "He got Marsha pregnant and you're going around school flaunting that you are sleeping with him" she yelled at me. "I'm not flaunting anything. He didn't get Marsha pregnant. Her brother did you dumbass" I said. Jaxon told me the truth. She didn't want anyone to know. They weren't really related. She was adopted. "Yeah right" the girl said dumping her drink all over my dress. My mouth opened. I looked up at her. Before I could do anything Bree pulled her back and punch the girl in the face. "I picked that dress out" she yelled after she punched her. Jaxon pulled me away from the scene and put the door. He pulled me to his car and opened the back. He pulled out a hoodie and I pulled it on. I got into his car. Bree came walking out and got into the back. Jaxon started to drive off. "Is it true?" She asked Jaxon. "Yeah. It's true. She doesn't want anyone knowing it was him so she picked me. The other guy she slept with" he said. She shook her head. Then she slapped the back of his head. "What the hell was that for?" He demanded. "For doing that to Lena" she said sitting back into her seat. He shook his head and I tried not to laugh at it. We went out to a diner and went inside.

We sat at a booth. I was next to Jaxon and she sat across from us. We ordered some food. "Look I'm still mad about the situation. You are my best friend and my brother" she said. "If it helps. Way before I left she was worried about it because of you and when I came back she said we couldn't. But I pushed her. I wanted to be with her again" Jax said. "I wanted to be with him too" I added. "When did this all happen?" She asked. I smiled at it. "Remember the beach party?" Jaxon said. "Yeah what about it?" She replied. "Well Lena got boobs that year and a butt. Not fully developed obviously. And I actually noticed her more than just my little sisters friend. That night when we had the fire later on at our house she went inside to get a drink. I followed her in and I kissed her. I said that I like you and it started from that" he responded. "So you guys have been together since that party?" She asked. "We weren't togeth-er when I went away" he answered. "We said our byes the day he left" I added. "So what about when you came back?" She asked. "That night he came back I woke up. Thirsty and had to go to the bathroom. I went downstairs and he kissed me down there" I answered. "I'm not going to apologize for falling for him. I love your brother" I added. "And I love her" he said. "You don't have to apologize. Mom talked to me last night. Told me the way I was acting was immature and said I'm allowed to be angry about it but I had to realize it was my best friend and my brother" she replied. We nodded. The waitress came over and set the food in front of us.

Later on Jaxon pulled up in front of their house. "Are you coming in?" She asked. "No I'm go-ing back home" I answered. "Are you coming home tonight?" She replied. "Probably not" he responded looking at me. She nodded. "Gross" she said getting out. I laughed. We waited to leave until she was inside the house. He drove us to my house. Jaxon went up to my room and I went to the kitchen. There was a note and some money. I didn't even know my mom came home. It was note saying she just got home and had to go on another trip. This time she left two hundred. I grabbed the money and went upstairs to my room. I went to the closet and grabbed the box. He came into my closet. "Where did you get all that?" He asked looking at the bag with all the money. "Mom and dad" I answered. "That's gotta be over a thousand there" he replied. I nodded. "Over five" I responded. "What are you saving that for?" He asked. "Don't know" I answered. He nodded. I put the box back and took the dress off. I went into my bathroom with him following me. I cleaned off all the sticky punch from my skin and looked at him. I smiled. He laughed. He came out of the bathroom with me following him. He took the coat off to the tux. He took the long sleeved shirt off. I grabbed it and put it on. I didn't even button it. He pulled me to him and kissed me. I pushed him back on the bed and climbed on top of him. I kissed him back.

Chapter 13

I woke up happy. Jaxon has his head on my chest and I started playing with his hair. He kissed my chest and looked up at me. "I can't wait for my birthday. When I have my own place. We could do this every morning" he said. I smiled. "We kind of are already doing this every morning" I replied. "Yeah but if we had a place imagine what we could do in every room" he responded kissing my neck. I laughed. He pulled away and smiled. "You're birthday isn't for a month" I said. He nodded. "Yeah. Wish it was sooner" he replied. He sat up and leaned against the headboard. I sat up too and he pulled me onto his lap.

I put my hands on his sides and he wrapped his arms around me. "I love you" He said looking me in the eyes. "And I love you" I replied. He lightly smiled and kissed me. I brought my hands up to his face. I kissed him back and he pulled me closer. He put his hands on my sides. I didn't even bother buttoning up the shirt last night before I went to bed. That was when my bedroom door opened. Bree walks in and stopped. "Gross" she said. "Bree can you give us a little privacy?" Jax said. "No. I need to catch up on time with Lena. You can have her anytime. But right now I want a girls day" she replied. He sighed. I got off of his lap and walked over to Bree. I grabbed a frozen latte and took a drink. "Bree I need you to leave so I can get dressed please" Jaxon said. She nodded and left the room. I turned towards him and he opened his arms. I put the drink down and hopped back onto his lap. He rolled us over to where he was on top. He attacked my neck with kisses. I laughed and pushed him away. I pulled his head down and kissed him. "I'm coming in in two minutes" Bree yelled from outside the door.

He groaned and grabbed one of my pillows. He tossed it at the door.

I walked Jaxon to the door. He kissed me and I kissed him back. He pulled away. "I'll call you later tonight" he said. I nodded. He kissed my forehead and left. I stood at the door and watched him drive off. I closed the door and went into the living room. "You could've put clothes on" she said looking at me. I was still only wearing his dress shirt just buttoned up this time. "Hey it's my house and I can wear what I want. Plus I can still smell him on this" I replied sticking my tongue out at her. She shook her head. I sat down on the couch. "So. What are we doing today?" I asked. "Well I thought we could order food and watch some movies like old times" she answered. "How about we call Jaxon to get our food and deliver it?" I suggested. "Right. Smart idea" she said. She grabbed her phone and then looked at me. "Do you want to call him?" She asked. I nodded and got up to get my phone. I grabbed it and called him. "Miss me already?" He asked. "Yes. But I got a favor to ask you" I answered. "What's that?" He replied. "Can you pick up some food for us. I don't want to order out" I responded. "Anything for you babe. I'll be there in maybe twenty minutes to half an hour" he said. "Thank you" I replied. "I love you" He responded. "I love you" I said. We hung up and I went to the living room. She was already on Netflix looking for something to watch.

The door bell rang and I went to get it. I opened the door and pulled him in for a kiss. "Hottest delivery man ever" I said. He laughed. He set the bags down by the door on the floor and pulled me closer to him. He crushed his mouth against mine and bent me back a little bit. "Get a room" Bree yelled. We broke apart. "We had one earlier until someone wanted to barge in" he said. I laughed. He kissed me one more time. "If you need anything else. Call me" he replied. I nodded. "Bree you have to be home by 8. Dad said" he added. She nodded. "Bye babe" he said. "Bye" I said smiling. He walked out the door. I grabbed the food and went into the living room. "Guessing you have a curfew instead of being grounded?" I asked. "Yup sucks money balls" she answered. I laughed.

Chapter 14

"Come over" I said. "Let me shower and I'll be right there" he replied. "Okay but please hurry" I responded. "I will" he said. We got off of the phone. I cleaned up the living room and took the leftovers to the kitchen. I put them in the fridge and grabbed a water. I was about to go upstairs when someone knocked on my door. I went to get it. I opened the door expecting Jaxon but it wasn't him. It was Marsha. She pushed passed me and looked around. "What are you doing?" I asked. "I'm looking for Jaxon. You know. The father of my child" she answered. She looked at what I was wearing.

"Do you always answer the door wearing a shirt?" She added. "Marsha stop. Jaxon is not the father to your child. He did a DNA test. It was negative. You shouldn't have slept with your brother even if he's not your blood relation" I said. She turned towards me and slapped me hard. I looked at her and glared. "What the hell is up with everyone slapping me lately" I yelled. "Get out of my house" I added. "I want my baby daddy" she said. "Then go home" I replied. "Would you shut up already. I know he's here. You're wearing his shirt" she responded going further in my house. The door opened and Jaxon came in. "Get her out of here now" I demanded. He looked behind me and saw what I meant. "Marsha what are you doing here?" He asked. "Looking for you" she answered coming closer. "Why?" He replied. "Because my child needs its daddy" she responded. "We've been over this. I'm not the father. You even told me you slept with someone a week before we dated also when we had sex. I used a condom. It didn't break and it was brand new.

Wasn't in my wallet. Nothing. We went to the store and bought them then used one right after. We didn't even make it back to my room" he yelled. "Explain this" she said pointing to her stomach. I went over to her and ripped her shirt up. It was a fake bump. She slapped me harder than the first time and I fell to the ground. I tripped her and she went down. Jaxon helped me up. She looked up. "You're suppose to be helping me" she screamed. "I'm not helping a lying bitch who fakes a pregnancy" he yelled back. She got up and got into his face. I pushed her back. She punched me in the stomach and I leaned forward holding my stomach. I stood up slowly and grabbed her by her hair and I pushed her to the door. Jaxon opened the door and I threw her out. "Never come back" I yelled. I slammed the door and walked in the house more. I went into the bathroom and looked in the mirror. I was definitely going to have a bruise on my cheek. I grabbed a towel and got it wet. I put it to my mouth because the split that was there before hand opened.

I came out of the bathroom and he was standing in the middle of the hallway. "All this drama because of me" he said. "It's fine" I replied. I started going up the steps and he didn't follow me. I turned and looked at him. "Lena you keep getting hurt because of me. She's going to get back at us for this. You just exposed her" he responded. "Jax whatever happens happens. To me. It's all worth being with you. I finally get you after you being away for a little over a year. I can handle this. I don't need you giving up after we got to this point in our lives" I said. "I think we should take a break for a little bit" he said. That was when my heart dropped. I didn't hear anything else he was saying. He just broke up with me. I ran upstairs and closed my door. I started to breath a little harder. I put my hands in my hair. I wanted to scream and cry at the same time. I was a little angry and hurt too. I went to my bathroom and punched the mirror.

Chapter 15

"Can believe you broke your wrist" Bree said. I shrugged. We were getting ready for a party. Her parents let her stay the night. I put on my tights with short shorts. I grabbed the same vest I had her wear the first party we went to with Jaxon. It made my chest area pop out a little extra. And showed off more skin on me. I buttoned two buttons out of four. I lightly curled my hair. "Ready?" I asked. She nodded. She drove us to the woods. We got out and walked to every-one. The fire was going and everyone was get-ting wasted. I saw Jaxon sitting with his friends. I walked by to get to the drinks. Bree was walking with me. I grabbed a drink with my good hand and chugged it. I got another one and turned around. He was watching me. I rolled my eyes and took another drink. "I'm just doing water tonight since I'm driving" she said. I nodded. I finished my drink. I went to the fire and threw the cup in it. I grabbed Bree's hand and we went to dance. After dancing for a little bit I went to get a drink. I grabbed a cup and someone pulled me away from there. I looked and saw Jaxon. "What are you doing here?" He asked. "It's a party. I'm came to party" I answered. He shook his head and looked down at what I was wearing. "You should go home" he replied. "Why?" I demanded. "Because you're here looking like that and what happened to your wrist" he replied. "None of your damn business anymore" I responded. I took a step and he grabbed me. "Jaxon what do you want from me? You broke my heart" I demanded pushing him. I got my drink on his shirt when I did. It didn't even faze him. He grabbed my waist and pulled me to him. "Lena I love you. I don't want you getting hurt anymore" he said.

"If you loved me. You wouldn't have broken up with me no matter what. I can handle myself. I've been doing it for a long time" I replied. "Please just go home" he responded. I shook my head. I backed away from him and went to get another drink.

I didn't feel good. I had a lot to drink. Bree was helping me walk back to her car. Jaxon came over and picked me up. "Put me down" I whined. "Lena what's going on with you? You never drink like this" Bree said. I tried getting out of his arms. "Stop fighting me" he whispered in my ear. He put me in the back of the car. It wasn't Bree's car. "Take your time going to her house. I'm gonna try to sober her up" he said to her. She nodded and got into her car. He got in the front and started driving. We got to my house and he carried me inside. He took me upstairs to my room and right into the bathroom. He set me down on the toilet. And looked at the mirror. I didn't replace it yet. Or clean up the mess. He shook his head and turned the bath tub on. He started unbuttoning my vest and I pushed his hands away. "Babe stop" he said. I wanted to cry and I did start crying. He wiped some tears away. "You broke my heart" I said. "I know and I'm sorry" he replied. He pulled me to his chest. I pushed him away and quickly got off the toilet. I threw up. He held my hair and rubbed my back. I sat down on the floor and flushed the toilet. He helped me up. He took his shirt off and got down to his boxers. He took my vest off of me and pulled my shorts along with my tights down. I stepped out of them and he got into the tub. He pulled my hand for me to join him. I got in and sat facing away from him. "Come here" He said holding his arms open. I went into them and he held me kissing my forehead. I closed my eyes. I didn't care that my cast was getting wet. Or that when we get out he's going to leave me. I just needed this. He bent his head down and kissed me. I kissed him back and pulled a little on his hair. He moved me to where I was straddling him. I pressed my chest against his.

We came out of the bathroom and I sat down on my bed. He let me wear his shirt that he wore earlier. He pulled my blanket back and I moved up and got underneath them. He went to his phone and messaged someone real quick. He got in the bed next to me. I snuggled into him more.

Chapter 16

I woke up and my head was pounding. I groaned and sat up. I got out of bed and went to my bathroom. I grabbed some aspirin. I took two and went back to my room. Jaxon was sitting at the end in only his jeans. "You don't have to pity me anymore. You can go home" I said. I went to the bed and got back under the blanket. He moved back to me. "I'm not taking pity on you. I love you Lena. I'm not going anywhere. Last night. I saw how bad it was for you. It's bad for me too. It's hard staying away from you. I can't do it" he replied. I looked at him. "We took a break for a day and I couldn't do it. I wanted to call you and come over every minute after it happened. I'm sorry babe. Please forgive me" he added. "I love you Jax. Please don't ever do that again" I replied. He nodded and pulled me into his arms. He pulled away from me. "I'm going to clean up the bathroom" he said. "Why?" I asked. "Because there is broken glass all over the sink" he answered. "I'll clean that up" I replied getting out of bed. "Babe. Relax. I can do it. I'll also get another mirror for you later today" he responded. I shook my head and then remembered. "Where's Aubrey?" I asked. "She's sleeping in the guest room" he answered. I nodded. I went to the bathroom and he followed me. I grabbed a towel and started moving the glass to the edge of the sink. He stopped me and took the towel. "I got it" he said. I shook my head and went to the bed. I sat down on it and he soon he came back out. He came over to me and pulled me to the edge of the bed. "Next time you wanna hit something because of something I did. Please let that be a pillow or even me" he said. "I don't want to hit you" I replied. "Please" he responded. I nodded.

He pushed my hair behind my ear. He pushed me back against the bed smiling.

About an hour later Bree knocked on the door and came in. "I see you guys made up" she said. We were both under the blanket. Thank god. She's seen me in my bra and underwear before but not completely naked. I sat up holding the blanket to my chest. "I just came to say mom and dad want us home. They wanna have a family day" she said. "Okay. Tell them I'll be there soon" Jax replied. She nodded and left the room. I laid back on the bed. "That was close" I said. He laughed. Jaxon left twenty minutes later. He said he would call me when he was able to and that he would be back over tonight. That left me completely alone in this house. I went into my bathroom and took down the mirror. I took it out to the trash. I grabbed my bag and went to the store to buy a new one. After I bought one I went to get something to eat. I got a sub and ate it while I was walking around outside. I came back to the house and put it up in my bathroom. By the time I was done it was around five. I went back into my room and stripped out of my clothes. I went to the closet and grabbed one of Jaxon's shirts that he left here last week. I put it on and came out of the closet. I laid down on my bed but only after turning Netflix on the tv. I put a horror movie on. All that was left for me to do is wait for Jaxon to come.

I woke up to him getting in the bed. I looked at the time and it was ten. "Sorry I didn't mean to wake you" he said. "It's okay. How was family day?" I asked. "It was okay. We went to the movies and out to the mall. Bree had fun because she got a lot of new stuff" he answered. "She always has to get something if you take her to the mall" I replied. He laughed. "You're not wrong there" he responded. "I got a new mirror" I said. "I told you I would do that for you" he replied. "I know but you've also replaced my window two times" I responded. "Because it was my fault they broke" he said. "And the mirror was mine" I replied. "Not technically" he responded. "Let's just let it go" I said. He nodded and smiled at me. "What were you watching on Netflix?" He asked. "I did watch a creepy clown movie and then it went to the walking dead" I answered. "Wanna watch some more with me?" He replied. "Anytime" I responded. I put the walking dead back on and snuggled into him.

Chapter 17

My head snapped to the right and I fell back into the lockers. I turned back and swung my good wrist knocking it into her face. The other girl came running at me and tackled me to the ground. I groaned when I hit the floor. She was on top of me and felt super heavy. I pushed her off of me and climbed up on top of her. I punched her in the face repeatedly. The first girl grabbed my hair and pulled me back it. I yelled. Two on one. Always bad. She stopped until I was on the ground. She started to punch me. I used my bad wrist with the cast and punched upward. She stopped punching me and fell to the ground next to me. She was out cold. The other girl crawled over to me to take that girls place. Someone ripped her off of me. It was a teacher. Another one pulled me up off of the ground. There was blood everywhere. "That's enough" the teacher yelled. "They started it. I was just defending my-self" I said holding my hands up. The teacher let me go. The other teacher holding that girl let her go and she tried coming at me again. Both teachers grabbed her. "I don't care who started what. My office now" the principal said coming closer to us. "Get this girl to the nurse" he said. One of the teachers got the girl who was knocked out and took her to the nurses off. We both walked out of the girls locker room. Everyone was watching and I mean everyone. Jaxon was standing at his locker with wide eyes. Bree was standing by the door when we walked out. She ended up walking over to him.

The three of us got suspended. I was just defending myself against Marsha's little friends that attacked me in the girls locker room. What was I suppose to do? Take it? I don't think so. They called my parents. Of course no one answered. My mom was on a business trip. My dad was busy with his new family. They had no other choice but to call Jaxon's parents who were listed in my file. Their mom came to get me. She also pulled Bree and Jaxon from school when she got here. A parent had to come get the child that got in trouble. Ironic since I barely had parents now. Bree got in her moms car and I got into Jaxon's car. "Nice job by the way" he said looking at the road. "What do you mean?" I asked. "You didn't break your other wrist" he answered smiling. I laughed. "Bitches had it coming. I mean jumping me when I was done with gym. Come on" I replied. "Oldest one in the book" he responded. "I know" I said. He grabbed my hand. "Your face is going to be bruised up tomorrow" he replied. "Yeah but it was worth it" I responded. He nodded. He pulled into his drive way after his mom. We got out and went into the house. "Lena I need to talk to you" she said. We went into the kitchen. "I'm not mad. You were defending yourself against those girls.

But sweetie try to take a less violent way at doing it" she said. I nodded.

Bree and I were sitting on the couch watching tv. Or she was flipping through the channels. I had my phone out looking on Facebook. "I'm so bored" she said throwing the remote on the other couch. "There's pretty much nothing we can do though" I replied. She nodded. I put my phone down on my lap. "Maybe we can go play in Walmart?" She suggested. "Yeah but I don't know if your parents are gonna let me out" I responded. She rolled her eyes. "They will" she said. She got up and turned the tv off. "Let's go" she added. I nodded. She grabbed the car keys and we went to the car. We got to Walmart and she got on one of those elderly carts for those who can't walk long. I laughed when she crashed it into the wall. I laughed harder when one of the workers came running over. She hopped off of it and ran. I ran with her. They didn't follow us. We went into the furniture section and she grabbed a bean bag off of the top shelf. I stepped on the bottom shelf and pulled one down myself.

We set them down and took a seat. She let out a sigh. I laughed. "Never tell anyone about that" she said smiling. I nodded. "It was funny as hell though" I replied. She nodded and shrugged. I leaned back and took my phone out of my pocket. "Still nothing from Jax?" She asked. "No" I answered. "He only left for the party an hour and a half ago" she replied. "I know. It sucks your mom said no when he asked if I wanted to go" I responded. "My mom can be tough. Like you're kind of her kid too. You go into trouble and the school called her. Your mom was smart to put her down as another contact for you" she said. I shrugged. "Even if my mom answered that call. She would've been to busy to care" I replied. "And your dad has another family to care too. I swear I don't ever wanna end up like our own parents" she responded. I nodded. "Wanna crash the party?" She asked smiling at me. I smiled back and nodded. She jumped up and grabbed my hand. "Let's go" she said pulling me away. "What about the bean bags?" I said as we were walking. "Leave them. I can't lift that back up and neither can you" she replied. I shrugged and we went to the car.

We pulled up to the party and it was a bigger fire than usual. We got out and went to get a drink. We both grabbed waters and sat down on a log near the fire. I looked around and didn't see Jaxon anywhere. His friends were standing near the drinks getting new ones. I looked back near the cars and could see his. "I don't see him" I said. She looked around. "His car is here. Maybe he went to the bathroom" she replied shrugging. I nodded. "You can drink. I'm definitely driving back so" she added. I nodded and went to get an actual drink. I grabbed a solo cup. I turned and miles and Nelson gave me a light smile. I smiled back. I walked over to them. "Hey guys what's going on?" I asked. "Nothing" they both answered at the same time. "Have you seen Jaxon?" I asked. "Nope" they both said again. I frowned. Since when did they start talking like that together. I shook my head and went to walk towards Bree when I saw it. Jaxon was leaning against a tree with a girl in front of him. He was smiling and laughing. She leaned forward and kissed him. He didn't push her away. My mouth opened. Bree came over to me and saw what I did. She grabbed my drink from my hand and walked over there. She tapped on his shoulder and they pulled apart. His eyes grew wide. She tossed the drink in his face. Then she turned towards me. He looked and he tried following his sister over here but she turned around pushing him hard onto the ground.

Chapter 18

W e didn't go back to the house or mine. We went to the playground we use to play at when we were kids. I sat down on the swing and she sat down next to me. "Are you okay?" She asked. "Well it's not every day you see your boyfriend kissing another girl" I replied. She shook her head. "I'm not taking you to one of our houses tonight in case he tries to get to you. I think ignoring him would he the best idea" she responded. I nodded and handing her my phone. She took it and put it in her pocket.

I woke up and my back was hurting. I looked over at Bree. She was still sleeping. I slapped her arm and she jumped up. "We should get going" I said. She nodded and put her seat up."I'm hungry. So we are stopping for food" she said. I nodded. She drive us to McDonald's. We got out and went inside. We ordered food and I went into the bathroom. I looked into the mirror at myself. Never have I ever imagined I'd be the girl who got cheated on by her two year relationship. I shook my head. I came out and sat down across from Bree who was biting into her sandwich. I grabbed mine and started eating.

Bree handed me my phone and I took it. I got out of her car and went into my house. I ran upstairs and sat down on my bed. I turned my phone on and it was going off non stop. Messages and calls from Jaxon. I rolled my eyes and turned my phone off again when he was trying to call me again. I got off of the bed and grabbed a bag. I put my phone in it and grabbed some money from my closet along with putting some clothes in the bag. I walked out of my room and outside of the house. I went to my car and Jaxon pulled up behind mine. I turned to look at him when he got out. "Lena let me explain please" he said. "Move your fucking car" I replied. I ripped my door open and got inside. "Please" He said. I shook my head and started my car. He didn't move. I groaned and looked at the distance between our cars. I backed up and took a deep breath. My mom was going to kill me. I pulled out in the front yard and got on the road leaving him behind standing in my drive way.

The next day I rushed to school. I was staying in a hotel room so he couldn't break into my room. I ran into the school and to my locker. I grabbed my first period book and turned around quickly bumping into a chest. I looked up and saw Jaxon. "I'm late. Move" I said. He wouldn't let me past him. I groaned. "Do you really wanna do this now? When I'm in a rush and a little irritated?" I demanded. "We need to talk" he said. "Fine. Here it is. You cheated. We're done. Now move" I replied. "Lean" He responded. I pushed passed him and ran to my class that I was already late for because of him. I could've made it on time if he didn't stop me. I groaned because I got detention. After I got out of detention I went to the Chinese restaurant that Bree wanted me to meet her at. I walked in and saw her. I went over to her and sat down. She slid the drink she got me and I grabbed it. "How was detention?" She asked. I glared at her. She laughed. "Your brother is the reason why I have it" I answered. "I know and I apologize for him" she replied. I shook my head. "I'm getting some food" I responded. I got up and went to the food. I sat back down and started to eat. Bree was looking on her phone. "Party this weekend?" She asked. "Sure. My mom isn't going to be back until Monday. I'm gonna talk to her about maybe getting my own place. To do that. I have to have her sign me off. Along with my dad" I answered. "Don't do that" she replied. "Why not?" I responded. "Because if you do then how are you going to afford it?" She said. I didn't tell her about the little stash I had. "I'll get a job" I replied. "Along with going to school? You won't be able to do it" she responded. I shrugged. "Guess you're right" I said.

Chapter 19

B ree and I were getting ready for the party. I put on a pair of faded skinny jeans that had little rips in them. I put on a black v neck shirt that hugged my body perfectly. I tucked it into the jeans. I put on my boots. I tossed my hair up into a pony tale. I put on some bold make up. I looked at Bree. She was wearing skinny jeans and a button up flannel along with her vans. I smiled. I gave her a thumbs up. She grabbed two hoodies from the closet. "It's getting colder out" she said. I nodded. I grabbed my phone and put it in my back pocket.

We got to the party. Same spot as always. You'd think they'd move it to a house when it gets a little nippy out but nope. Only when there's snow on the ground where they can't do a fire. We walked over to get drinks. I took mine and downed it. I downed a few more. I grabbed one more and we went to dance. I had about four drinks in me already while Bree hasn't even finished her first. I swayed to the music and drank some more. "Girl you're not driving tonight" Bree said. I nodded and pulled my keys out from my pocket. I handed them to her. She took them and put them in her pockets. "I just wanna have fun and forget the world" I said smiling and dancing. She laughed. "Then lets get you to do it" she replied. She handed me the rest of her drink and I downed that. I threw the cup in the fire. Someone came by me and pushed me hard on the ground. I scrapped my hands for sure. I looked up and glared at Marsha.

She laughed. She wasn't sporting the baby bump anymore. I stood up and pushed her to the ground. "Don't fucking touch me" I yelled. Bree pushed me away from her and we went back to dancing. "She has no friends anymore after you exposed her for lying and faking a pregnancy" she said. "Like I care about that. She's a bitch. She needs to be put in her place" I replied. "Don't do it while you're drunk. Remember you want to forget the world and have some fun. Don't let her ruin that for you" she responded. "Why are you okay with me doing this?" I asked. "Because after the week you had. You need it" she answered shrugging. I nodded. I looked over to where he usually sat and saw him. He was watching me with a drink in his hand. I looked away. I had about eight drinks and could feel it. But I didn't care. I wanted to have fun. A lot of fun. I saw some guys take out some stuff. I walked closer and saw that it was a brownie. I went over to them. "Can I have one?" I asked. The guy nodded and gave one to me. I took a big bite into it. "Just one though.

If you eat more you're gonna regret it" He said. I frowned and then shrugged. I walked away. I ate almost all of it when Bree knocked it out of my hands. I poured. "Honey that's a pot brownie" she said. Shit. "I didn't know" I replied. I spit out what was in my mouth. "It's too late. You already ate almost all of it" she said. I groaned. "Fucking stoners" I replied. I walked over to get another drink and downed it again. I started to feel the effects. I laughed at pretty much everything. Along with feeling hungry. Also tired. I sat down on a chair and pulled the hoodie on. Bree went and got them not that long ago. I leaned back in the chair and closed my eyes. I felt someone grabbed me. I was too tired to open my eyes. I felt cold after a few minutes. Then I heard screams and yells. Then came some grunts and groans. I opened my eyes when someone lifted my back up off of the ground. I saw a foot ball jock on the ground and Jaxon on top of him.

I noticed my legs were bare. Jaxon came over to us and picked me up bridal style. He carried me around the party so no one would see and into my car. "Are you going to be okay driving?" He demanded. "Yes. I only had a few sips" she replied. He groaned. "I'll meet you at her house to get her in the house" he responded. "I don't need your help" I said. "Yes you do" Bree snapped. I rolled my eyes. I turned on my side in the back seat. He closed the door. I could see them yelling at each other. I closed my eyes not caring.

Chapter 20

When I woke up this morning I felt refreshed until I had to run to the bathroom. I threw up everything in my system. I walked back to my room and noticed I was only in my sports bra and underwear. I looked around the room and didn't see my clothes from last night. I shrugged and went downstairs. I went into the kitchen and grabbed some juice. I took a big long drink. I jumped when someone cleared their throat. I looked and saw Jaxon standing against the door frame. "What are you doing here?" I asked. "I brought you in last night. Don't worry Bree changed you. She didn't finish because you threw up on her twice. She left after. I stayed.

I wanted to know you were okay" he answered. "I don't need you here" I replied. "Lena. Do you realize how bad last night was? All because you wanted to have some fun? You almost got raped. Again. All because you had to get drunk and eat a fucking pot brownie without thinking about what I told you the first time I ever took you to a damn party. Never take drinks from someone. Do not eat foods from the stoner kids" he yelled. "I'm fine. I've been doing okay without you in my life. You cheated on me and now you're in my house. Thinking it's okay. Just leave me alone" I yelled back. I went to him and started pushing him out of the kitchen but he wouldn't move."Get out" I screamed pushing his chest. He wouldn't budge. He wrapped his arms around me and pulled me tight. I couldn't move back. "I was drunk. I didn't mean to do it. I made a stupid idiot choice and I'm sorry. I know that doesn't make it okay. I know.

But honestly. Lena. I love you. I only want to be with you. I want to stay it won't happen again.

I want you to trust me. I want you to believe in me. You've always believed in me. Even when all I did was get in trouble. You never once treated me differently. I swear on my life I will never ever hurt you again. Please" he said as I kept trying to get out of his arms. "Let me go" I begged. I was starting to cry. "Never" He said. He finally let me go. He pushed my hair back from my face. He tucked it behind my ears. I would look at him. I slapped him. His head turned to the side. I pushed him again. He grabbed my arms pulled me to his chest. I looked up at him and he kissed me. I didn't kiss him back. He kept kissing me. It took me a minute to kiss him back. He bent down a little bit. His hands on the back of my thighs. He lifted me up and I wrapped my legs around his waist. I wrapped my arms around his neck. He walked me over to the table and set me down.

I couldn't believe I did that. I looked at him. He was breathing a little hard. I locked my lips and looked back up at the ceiling. I sat up. I got down from the table. I grabbed my bra and underwear. I put them on. I grabbed his clothes from the ground and threw them at him. He sat up. "What's going on?" He asked. "You need to leave" I answered. I walked out of the kitchen. He came after me and grabbed my arm. "But we just had sex" he said. "Yeah and we shouldn't have done that. You cheated. Why on earth would I forgive you for that?" I demanded. "Because you love me and I love you" He replied. I shook my head. "Yes I love you but you broke my heart again" I responded. I pulled my arm from his hold and went upstairs.

Later on that day I scrubbed and scrubbed the table. If my mom knew about it. I don't think she would ignore me anymore and be all in my business. My phone went off and I grabbed it. I answered it. "Wanna hang out?" Bree said. "Yeah. You can come over. Bring food with you. And I need to talk to you" I replied. "Got it. See you soon" she responded. We hung up the phone and I continued scrubbing the table. Bree came in with bags. I laughed. We brought them to the kitchen. "What's up with the table?" She asked. All the cleaning products were on there. Along

with my gloves."Jaxon and I had sex" I blurted."
On the table?" She said with wide eyes. "Maybe" I
replied. "Ew. So I'm guessing you did forgive him"
she responded. "No" I said. She smacked my arm.
"Why the hell did you do that with him then?"
She asked. "I don't know. We were fighting and
then he kissed me. Next thing I know we are on
the table" I answered. She nodded. "My brother
came back and he looked a little hopeful" she
replied. I shrugged.

Chapter 21

A week and a half passed since then. I went into school. I had my hood up and walking a little slow. I was cramping. I hated it. Came every month and I hated being a girl because of it. I got pulled into a closet. I looked and saw Jaxon. He pulled me into a kiss. I kissed him back. He pulled away and pulled my hoodie off. He smiled when he saw I was only wearing a bra underneath. He attacked my mouth with a bunch of kisses. We came out and I shook my head. I kept giving in to him. He knew it.that I wasn't going to deny him anymore for that anyways. That was the fourth time since the day after the party. I wasn't exactly on my period yet. I just had the cramps that came a few days before. I went to my locker and grabbed my books.

I went to Bree's house and we went to the living room. I threw my bag on the other couch. "Can I use one of your shirts?" I asked. She nodded. I went up to her room and took the hoodie off. I put on one of her tank tops. I came out of her room and Jaxon was there. He was walking to his room. He smirked when he saw me. He grabbed my arm and pulled me to his room. He kissed me and backed me up to the bed. He gently laid me back on it. Every time this happened this week he was being gentle when setting me back against something. When we were done I pulled my sweat pants up and put my tank top on. I looked at him. "We can't keep doing this" I said. He looked away. "Hopefully in a week or two you'll change your mind" he replied. "Why do you say that?" I asked. "You'll see" he answered. I shook my head and went downstairs. "Again?" She asked. I groaned and sat down next to her."I don't know why I can't stop" I said. "I think you guess are meant to be then. You can't stay away from him long" she replied. "Maybe it's lust" I responded. "Or love" she said shrugging. I glared at her for that. She laughed.

I came home that night. I my sides were killing me. I groaned and went to the bathroom. I ran a warm bath. I put a bath bomb in it. I got undressed and got in. I laid back and closed my eyes. I thought about Jaxon. I opened my eyes and bit my lip. I leaned over the tub and grabbed my phone. I made a call."Hello?" He answered. "Come over" I replied. I could image him smiling. "Be there in five" he responded. "I'm upstairs in the bathroom when you get here" I said. "Okay" He said. I hung up on him. I leaned back against the tub. He came into the bathroom and got undressed. I moved forward and he got in behind me. "What made you change your mind?" He asked moving my hair from my neck and started kissing it. I closed my eyes. "I just really need you" I said. He smiled against my neck.

I walked out of the bathroom in a towel and into my room. I got dressed and laid down on my bed on my stomach. Jaxon came in. "You probably shouldn't lay on your stomach right now" he said. I raised my eyebrows. "And why shouldn't I?" I asked. "You said you're cramping and back hurt a little bit. Thought maybe laying on your back would make it feel better" he answered. I nodded and moved to be laying down on my back. He went over to the tv and turned Netflix on. He came back over to me and sat down. I turned on my side and snuggled into his side. He wrapped his arms around me. "This still doesn't mean anything. I just need snuggles and of course your body at the moment" I said. I looked up at him and he was smirking. I frowned. I didn't know what he knew but I was getting curious as to what he was doing.

Chapter 22

Another week passed. My period didn't come. Probably because of how stressed I am or how many times Jaxon and I had sex. I don't know. I felt little mild cramps but it was fine. I put some skinny jeans on and a long sleeved v neck shirt. I put my hair up into a pony tail. I grabbed my coat. I went downstairs. I put my coat on and grabbed my bag. I walked to Bree's house. I walked in and went to the kitchen were she was along with Jaxon and their mom. She put down some eggs and sausage in front of me. I grabbed a muffin and a piece of cheese. I made a sandwich out of it. "Let's go" Bree said grabbing hers. I grabbed mine and followed her out the door.

It was lunch time. I went to get some food. I grabbed some and was walking to a table. Jaxon came over to me while I was walking. I stopped. I felt pain. A lot of pain I dropped my tray and wrapped my arms around my stomach. I cried out in pain and went down to the ground. Jaxon grabbed me. Bree ran over to me. "It hurts" I said crying.

I was laying in the hospital bed. Jaxon and Bree were sitting in the chairs. The doctor came in and I sat up a bit. "Everything is fine. The baby is fine. Your stress level went a little higher than normal" he said. "Wait what" I demanded. "You're going to be fine" he said. I looked at Jaxon and he was smirking. The not laying in my stomach. Saying it won't be like that in a few weeks. Him being gentle. All the sex. No period. But he's always worn a condom. I looked at Bree her mouth was wide open. She was looking at her brother.

I walked out of the hospital with Bree right behind me and of course Jaxon. "Babe slow down"

Jaxon said. I turned towards him. "You planned this" I yelled. He tried not to smile. I shook my head. "What happened to condoms?" I screamed in his face. "I haven't worn one not since the day after the party where you got high. I thought you knew. Cause it did feel so much better without it. Even you said so yourself" he said. "I didn't know you weren't wearing one and if I did I would've made you stop. I'm not ready to me a mom. I'm too young" I replied. "It's too late to abort it" he responded. I slapped him. "Stay away from me. I mean it" I yelled. I walked away. I was pissed off. Extremely pissed off. He ruined my life.

I walked into the house and saw my mom at the counter setting up her laptop. I went into the kitchen. "Mom" I said. "Hey what are you doing home right now?" She asked. "I was taken to the hospital" I answered. She looked at me."Wha t happened?" She demanded. "I'm pregnant" I said. She sat down. "How far along?" She replied. I shrugged. She nodded. "The dad?" She asked. "Jaxon" I answered. She nodded. "I'm gonna go to the store. I'll make dinner. A good one for the baby. Also invite his family over. We have a lot to talk about" she replied. I nodded. I texted Bree about wanting them all to come to dinner tonight.

They came. Bree said that they didn't tell their parents. That they decided not to right now but knowing my mom they will know by the end of the night. Jaxon and Bree went to sit down in the living room while my mom was exchanging pleasantries with their parents. I went into the kitchen and leaned against one of the counters. I crossed my arms. Bree came in and lightly smiled at me. "So when you said you were done with my brother. You didn't mean it?" She asked. "I did but when I told my mom she wanted you guys over for dinner" I answered. "Do you want it?" She replied. "I honestly don't know what I want right now" I responded. She nodded. "You know Jaxon was an idiot for what he did. But he did it so he could try to keep you in his life.

More than his little sisters best friend. And this baby I think it's a blessing. All babies are. So if you want to keep it. Just know. You have me behind you a hundred percent. I know you can handle this baby and school" she said. I took a deep breath. "I can't even wrap my mind around this without being pissed off at Jaxon. He planned on his. I bet he thought. 'Hey if I can ever have sex with her again I'm gonna get her pregnant so she definitely won't leave me' I mean come on. Did he not think this through" I replied. "He probably didn't think it through" she responded. I nodded.We all sat down around the table. I sat by Bree. Jaxon sat across from me by his mom and dad. We started to eat. "So we have something serious to talk about right now" My mom said grabbing her glass of wine. "About?" Their dad asked. "Jaxon and Lena" My mom said. "Oh we already know. It's sweet. They've been dating for awhile" their mom said. "You think this situation is sweet?" My mom asked with raised eyebrows. "Yeah. They are perfect together" their mom said. "Let me get this straight. You think that since they are perfect together they are okay with raising a baby in high school?" My mom replied. Dead silent. I looked at their faces. His mom was shocked. Mouth open and eyes wide. Their dad was shaking his head and put his fork down. He picked up his beer and started drinking it.

"Jaxon did you not learn a thing from over the summer?" His dad demanded. "I did and honestly. If I were to have a baby. I'd rather it be with Lena" Jax said. I shook my head. "You planned on getting her pregnant without her even knowing about it" My mom responded. "Jaxon" his mom said shaking her head. "Look what's done is done" Jax replied. He looked at me and lightly smiled. I shook my head again. I wanted to slap him. "I can't believe you. Jaxon you called me during the summer about to shit your pants. That girl who claimed to be pregnant by you. You said you didn't want one. That the time was way wrong for you.

Why. Why on earth did you do this?" His dad asked. "Lena broke up with me. She saw me kiss another girl. When she would even kiss me I came up with it right on the spot and I made the choice" he answered. "You ruined everything by that" I yelled. They all looked at me. "You graduate this year. You're going to college. Me? I still have a year and half left of school. You blew my chances at college. Getting a decent job to provide for myself. Put the window. Not to mention. There is already one pregnant girl in my grade. She walks alone in the halls now. With her head down. She eats alone. I heard her crying in the bathroom the other day. That girl is going to be me. I'll be bullied just like her. I'll be talked about for the next couple years. My life is over" I said. "You'll have me no matter what. To hell what those girls say" Bree said. I shook my head. "Jaxon. You're getting a job. After school. No more football practice.

No nothing. You are going to help provide for that child. Bree. I expect you to say by her side and help her through this. She is our best friend. Lena you've been like a second daughter to us. If you need anything. Anything at all. You can always come to us" their dad said. We all nodded. "Lena. I want you to get a weekend job. At least until you are six months along. I don't care if it's

only for a few hours a day. You can save that up.
I'll also help financially. But I want you to save up.
Babies are not cheap" my mom said. I nodded. I
looked at Bree and she smiled at me.

Chapter 23

"Guess who got a job?" Bree asked. "Jaxon?" I answered. "Yes. But I did too. Jaxon is working with my dad. I got one with my mom at giant eagle" she said. "Why?" I replied. "Because. You're going to need a little help" she responded. "You don't need to do that" I said. She shrugged. "Deal with it" she replied. "I got a job at the book store" I responded. "That's good" she said. I nodded. We walked to the Chinese restaurant. We sat down at a table and did our drink orders. We got up and went to get some food.

Later on I went home. I went the kitchen and my mom was on her laptop. She held out an envelope. I grabbed it and opened it. There was cash. My mouth opened. "Mom what's this for?" I asked. "We started two saving accounts for you when you were born. One for college and one in case you ever needed it. It's not all that's in there but it's some of it. There's two thousand there" she answered. I went upstairs and put it with my other money. I grabbed some clothes and went in to shower.

I came out and Jaxon was sitting on my bed. "What are you doing here?" I asked. "I came to check up on you. On us" he answered. "Jaxon you planned on getting me pregnant. How do you think we are doing?" I replied. He looked down at the ground. "I was stupid. I know. But can you please look at it the way I was" he responded. I sat down next to him on the bed. "Jaxon I need some tome to adjust to all of this. It's not fair to me" I said. "I know. If it makes you feel better I'm not going to college. I'm gonna work with my dad at his firm" he replied. "You need to go to college" I responded. He shook his head. "Think about our baby. That is the only thing we need to think about for now on" I said. He nodded. "Do you want the baby?" I asked. He looked at me. "Of course I do" he answered. I nodded. "Do you?" He replied. "I think so" I responded.

He nodded. "But you're not sure" he said. "Jax I'm not even seventeen. I get it. You want us together. But honestly. We were. We had sex so many times during that time. I can't stop being near you. Then you did this. I know. I should've realized you didn't have one on but I didn't because I trusted you to wear one. You've always worn one. This baby. I don't even know what to do. I want kids. But I don't want them right now" I replied. He nodded. "So we are back together?" He responded. "Nope" I said. He shook his head with a small smile. "I'm really stupid" he replied. I pushed him a little bit. "Let's just take this one day at a time. Then we can talk about it when we are both ready" I responded. He nodded.

Jaxon left after we had our talk. He was willing to give it time for us to be together again.

I took a deep breath and laid back on my bed. I put my hand on my stomach. "Mama doesn't know what she wants to do" I said. I groaned and got up. I went downstairs and went to the living room. I grabbed my coat and keys. I drove to the bookstore. I walked in and took my coat off. There was barely anyone in here. I went behind the counter and started to work. I was getting really tired so the manager let me go home early. When I walked into the door I went upstairs to my room. I stripped down to my underwear and grabbed a tank top. I put it on and went to the tv. I turned it on and went to Netflix. I looked through some movies. I found to all the boys I've loved before and put it on. I paused it for a second and ran downstairs. I grabbed some snacks and a drink. My mom walked into the kitchen and raised an eyebrow when she saw that I had my arms full. I smiled at her and walked passed her shaking her head and trying not to laugh at me. I went back upstairs and made myself comfortable enough to play the movie.

Chapter 24

Christmas time came around. I was barely fitting into my clothes. I groaned at the dress I wear on Christmas. I could zip it up. Bree was trying to help me. "Maybe it's time to find a new one?" She suggested. I groaned again. "I'm sorry" she said. "It's not your fault. I'm gaining weight. And I have a baby bump" I replied. She shrugged. "You look good like that though" she responded. I took the dress off and pulled my sweat pants back on. I grabbed a shirt and put that on too. I pulled my hair back into a pony tail and looked at myself in my body mirror that hung on the wall. "Let's go get another dress" I said. She nodded.

We got to the mall and went into Macy's. I looked through the dresses and found one. I went to the dressing rooms and tried it on. It went a few inches above my knees.

It was a brown dress with lace for the upper part with the long sleeves and a little bit above the top part. It it was a maroon color and looked like it had a little sparkle to it. I smiled at it. I came out and Bree was standing there. "That dress is gorgeous on you" she said. We went to the mirror and I mostly focused on the baby bump. I put my hand on it. I saw a flash and looked towards it. Marsha. I groaned. "Who's a fat bitch now" she said. I was getting angry. I started walking towards her when Bree grabbed my arm. "Baby" she whispered. I took a deep breath and stood my ground. "What don't want I fight about it?" She taunted. I looked at Bree then at her. She was standing right in front of me. Bree pushes her back a bit. "Stand down. She doesn't need a body guard" Marsha hissed.

The next thing I know she throws a punch and I went to the floor with a little pain. I groaned.

"Lena" Bree yells turning towards me and getting down to the floor on her knees. She looked at Marsha. "You can't hit her" she added. Marsha shrugged and rushed out of the store before Bree or security got to her. She knew Bree would jump her for it since I didn't fight her back. I wish I did though. "Are you okay?" She asked. I nodded. "Lena you're bleeding" she added. I looked down on the ground. There was blood on my legs. I wanted to cry. She got her phone out. I started to cry when she was on it.

Another hospital trip. This time my mom was there. Bree called her when we were waiting for them to show up. "Is the baby okay?" My mom demanded when the doctor came in. "The baby is okay. Right now we want you to go home and relax. Bed rest for twenty fours hours. Then go to your doctor for a check up" he said. We nodded. My mom helped me down from the bed. I grabbed my coat. I was still in the dress from Macy's. Bree said she paid for it while she waited to the ambulance to show up. When we got home I went to my room and changed into the clothes

I had before. I laid down in bed and closed my eyes.I woke up when I heard my door open. Jaxon walked over to the bed. "Bree told me what happened" he said sitting down. "I'm fine. The baby is fine" I replied. He nodded. "Why didn't you call me? Or Bree?" He asked. "You were at work" I answered. "So? That doesn't mean you can't call and tell me" he was angry. I sat up. "If you're gonna be pissy with me leave. I'm not dealing with that tonight" I said. He shook his head and got up. He left and slammed the door behind him. I shook my head. I got up from the bed and went over to my tv. I turned it on. I sat down on my bed. I was mad. I don't think that I had to tell him everything that has happened during the day. Yes. I could've lost the baby today but I didn't. Nothing bad had happened to the baby. I groaned.

Chapter 25

I got the cast off of my wrist. I was showing more now. I've barely talked to Jaxon. He was suppose to bring me home from work tonight so we could talk. My mom was driving me back to school. I got out and grabbed my bag. I walked into the school. First day without a hoodie and everyone was able to see my bump. I didn't care that much if they did anymore. I walked in and went to the cafeteria. I got in line and got some food. Everyone was looking at me. I shook my head and went to sit down with Bree. She was stuffing her face. I laughed. "Shut up I'm starving. I woke up late and didn't have time to eat breakfast" she said. I nodded. I sat down and started eating. "Nice wrist" she commented. I laughed again. "It's a nice wrist isn't it?" I joked. She laughed. "How's it been going?" I asked. "Good. I got some money saved up. I got the baby a few things. Which are in my car. You can grab them when I take you to work after school" she said. I nodded. "How are you?" She asked. "I'm okay. I haven't really talked to Jax. Other than asking him for a ride home tonight. He's angry with me that I didn't tell him about the incident a few weeks ago" I answered. "Yeah he was angry with me when I told him too. He mostly works and comes home grumpy. He will get over it. Just give him a little time" she said shrugging. I nodded. "Should I feel bad about it though?" I replied. "No. Not at all" she responded.

After school I went to Bree's car and she gave me a bag. I opened it. My mouth opened. It was a little security blanket. Along with a blanket. I took them out and saw some binkies and bottles. Along with some socks. I looked at Bree and pulled her into a hug. "You didn't have to do that"

I said. "Yes I did. It's my baby niece or nephew in there. I'm telling you this now. This baby will be spoiled by auntie b" she replied. I laughed. "You're the best" I responded giving her another hug. She hugged me back and I got into her car putting the bag on my lap.Before she took me to work we went through the Burger King drive thru. We got to the bookstore and sat in the car. We ate our food and relaxed a little bit. "Thanks for the food" I said. She nodded with her mouth full of food. I laughed at her. I grabbed my bags and went into the store.

I walked out of the store and didn't see Jaxon's car anywhere. I leaned against the building. I grabbed my phone and saw his text that he was running a little late. I put my phone away and hugged myself. It was freezing out tonight. I put my bags down away from the snow. I rubbed my eyes. I was feeling hungry. Soon his car pulled up and I got inside. He had a bag and gave it to me. I opened it. I smiled. I took out a sandwich and ate it. I ate some fries. "Bree said you were craving Burger King the last week" he said. I nodded.

"Can we talk about this?" He replied. "About?" I asked. "Whenever something happens with you or the baby can you please let me know? I don't want to be the last one to know from my sister" he answered."Fine I'll let you know whatever happens between me and the baby" I replied."Good" He said nodding his head. He was watching the road and going slow. It was snowing out now. He put his one hand on my thigh and glanced at me. "Pull over" I said. I put the bags in the back behind me. He pulled over to the side of the road. I unbuckled the seat belt and climbed over onto his lap. He pushed his seat back more and down. I kissed him. He kissed me back and grabbed my thighs. I smiled.

We got back into our seats. I put my seat belt on and he started driving again. He grabbed my hand with a smile on his face. "It's been months" he said. I smiled. "Yeah I know" I replied. He brought our hands to his mouth. He kissed my hand. He looked at me and stopped smiling. He moved quickly but not quick enough. I screamed when I felt the impact.

Chapter 26

It was the day after the worst day. Jaxon and I got into a car accident. The other car hit ice and lost control of his car hitting right into us on my side. Jaxon tried to protect me but he ended up breaking his hand on the impact. That was the worst of his injuries though. He got a few cuts on his face. I on the other hand. I lost the baby. The seat belt cut my shoulder but not bad. I had bruises all over my right side. The worst part of it. Was losing the baby for me. I was upset. Jaxon was too. He said he was taking him to court and suing him for what he had done to us. I didn't want to deal with it.

My mom brought me home. I went upstairs to my room. I looked in my body mirror. I shook my head and sat down on my bed. There was a knock on my door and Bree came in. "Hey" she said. "Hi" I replied. "How're you holding up?" She asked sitting down next to me. I shrugged. I didn't know what to say. "Everything's going to be okay. You and Jaxon will get through this" she said. "I know. I just feel a little numb right now" I replied. "That's the medication they gave you sweetie" my mom said coming in. She gave me some more of the medication. I shook my head. "I don't think I need that right now" I replied. "The doctor said to give you some more when you got home" she responded. I took a deep breath and took it. She smiled. "Bree why don't you take her out for a little bit?" She suggested. Bree nodded and lightly smiled at me. "No drinking please. I don't want to clean my vase out again" she added. Bree laughed. I didn't.

We came out of the movie theater and I still wasn't feeling much. People would look at us and whisper. I rolled my eyes. I put my hand on my stomach and rub it. The doctor said I would still have to give birth to it and it hurt me even worse. Giving birth to my dead child. I cried my eyes out when they said it. "Can we go to your house tonight?" I asked. Bree looked at me. "Yeah. Would you like to get some food first?" She answered. I nodded. Like usual. We went through a drive thru and went to her house. We got out and went inside. I saw Jaxon sitting on the couch drinking from the bottle. We went into the kitchen. "He hasn't stopped drinking since he got home from the hospital" she said. I looked towards the living room. I shook my head and went to him. I sat down next to him. "Jaxon?" I said. He looked at me and I could tell he was crying. "What are you doing here?" He asked. "I wanted to see you" I answered.

"Why? I killed our child. Put you in the hospital. I'm a waste of space" he replied looking away from me and taking another drink. I grabbed the bottle from him. I set it down on the stand near me. I got up and sat down on his lap facing him. I put my hands on his shoulders. "It wasn't your fault it was the other driver who hit ice. How could you have known that was going to happen?" I responded. He looked at the wall. I grabbed his face and made him look at me. "Jaxon I love you. Maybe when we are both ready. We can try again. I'm not mad at you" I said. He leaned his forehead against mine. I knew he was looking down at the bump. He started crying and I held him. If it wasn't for the medication I took I knew I would be crying with him. After awhile we went to his room and laid down on the bed. I snuggled into him. He wrapped his arms around me. "Please don't leave me" he said. I looked up at his face. "No matter how much we fight. I don't think I'll ever be able to" I replied. He kissed my forehead. "I want to be there" he said. "I know. You will be. But it's not gonna happen for a few more months" I replied. He nodded.

Chapter 27

I felt butterflies in my stomach. I shook my head. I didn't know why. I walked out of the bookstore with Bree standing there. She stopped and stared at my stomach. "Uh Lena. I think something moved in your stomach" she said. I looked down and and saw what she meant. "I think we need to go to the doctors" I said. She nodded. I called Jaxon and my mom on the way to the hospital. The tech put the gel on my stomach and moved the wand around. "Who told you the baby didn't make it?" She said. "A doctor here in the ER" I replied. She moved the wand around more. She moved the screen so I could see it more. "Does that look like he didn't make it?" She responded. It was a He. I looked at the screen and saw him moving around. My mouth opened. I looked at Bree and she was smiling. The accident was a month ago. Damn doctor. My mom came rushing in the room and looked at us. "What's wring?" She asked. I pointed to the screen and her mouth dropped. She started to cry. "It's a freaking miracle" she yelled. I nodded. She gave me a hug and then hugged Bree. "Where's Jaxon?" She asked. "He's at work but told me to call him if we knew anything" Bree answered. She nodded.

Later that night I was sitting on Jaxon's bed. I was holding a blue gift bag. He walked in and threw his jacket on his desk. He looked at me. "What's that?" He asked. I smiled. I tapped the bed next to me and he said down. I kissed his cheek and gave him the bag. He opened it. He pulled out a small blue teddy bear and the pictures of the baby from the ultra sound. He pulled out a onesie saying I love my daddy. He looked at me. "What is all of this?" He asked. "When I went to the doctors they did an ultrasound on me. I guess the doctor that examined me was wrong. The baby is alive. He's moving around and kicking me. Bree saw him move in my stomach. That's why we went" I answered. He looked at me with wide eyes. "Really?" He replied. I nodded and he pulled me to him. I wrapped my arms around his neck. He laid us back and kissed my stomach. "You said he?" He said. "He's a boy" I replied. He smiled even bigger. "We're suing that doctor" he responded."My mom is already on it" I said. "Good" he replied."My dad will help with it too" he added. I nodded.

We went over to his house and I sat down on the couch. Jaxon told his parents what happened while I turned the tv on. Bree came in and sat down next to me. She grabbed the remote and put on Netflix. She went to the 100 and played it. I leaned my head on her shoulder. "Jaxon is happy" she said. I nodded. "How come you came over? I thought you needed to rest up?" She asked. "Jaxon wanted to talk to your dad about what happened. He wants him to help with the case my moms doing against him" I answered. "But you needed some rest" she said. "I know but I'll be okay" I replied. She nodded."Bellamy is so hot and I hope one day him and Clarke get together" she said. "They probably will" I replied. She smiled. "I wish she got together with him instead of Finn" she responded. We continued talking about the show. After a few episodes I felt really tired. Jaxon came in and we went upstairs to his room. I grabbed one of his shirts and changed into it. I got into the bed and snuggled into the blankets. He came over after changing into some sweats and laid down next to me. He wrapped his arms around my waist. "I'm so tired" I said. "Get some sleep love" he replied kissing my shoulder. I turned to look at him. "I don't really want to go to bed yet" I responded. "What do you want to do?" He asked. I shrugged a little bit. He lightly smiled. "Wanna pick out some baby names?" He suggested. I smiled and nodded.

Chapter 28

I was in horrible pain. I hated it. I looked at Jaxon. He was holding my hand. I was pushing. I let out a little yell. "Don't yell" the nurse said. I wanted to punch her in the damn face. "Shut the fuck up" I yelled. She rolled her eyes. I felt the pain again. "Push" she said and I pushed. A little cry. I looked down. The doctor put him on my stomach while he clipped the cord. He was so tiny and red. He picked him up and handed him to the nurse. I was still in pain until the placenta came out. I watched the nurses with our son. Jaxon walked over there and was smiling down at him. I wanted him so bad in my arms. Finally they brought him over to me for the skin to skin. I smiled down at our baby boy. Jaxon kisses my forehead. "You did good babe" he said. I nodded and held on to him.

I was in the hospital for two more days after that. Then we finally went home. My mom helped get my room ready for when we came back. I laid down on the bed with him. He was sleeping. I yawned. I grabbed my phone and set it for two hours for when he would need his next feeding. I closed my eyes and fell asleep cuddling my little human. I woke up to the alarm and panicked. He wasn't next to me. I looked to the little chair to see Jaxon holding him and feeding him a bottle. I shook my head. "Your mom told me you pumped some milk and put it in the fridge before you laid down with him" he said. I nodded. "Kind of gave me a heart attack a second ago. Didn't know where he went" I replied. "Did you hear that? We scared your mommy" he whispered towards him. I shook my head. "Maybe we should move in together. Be together to take care of our son" he said. "Maybe" I replied shrugging. He nodded and looked down at him.

Everyone was coming over to my house for dinner and to spend some time with Mathias. I looked around the room at everyone crowding around me while I held him. I needed some space. I gave him to Bree and got up from the couch. I went to the kitchen and grabbed some water. I turned around and leaned against the counter near the sink. I took a drink and then put it down on the counter. I crossed my arms and took a deep breath. Jaxon came in and smiled at me. I smiled back. "Do you wanna go out for a bit?" He asked. I nodded. We went back into the living room. "They have him. I already asked them to watch Mathias" he said. I nodded. I have Mathias a kiss on the forehead and went with Jaxon.

We drove around for a bit and then we went into the drive thru at Wendy's. We got some food and he drove us to an apartment building. He grabbed our bag of food and got out. I followed him. We went up to the second floor and he opened up a door. I stepped in and looked around. "What is this place?" I asked. "It's our place. It has two bedrooms. I got it last week for us and after today. I think maybe we could move in together like I said earlier" he answered. I nodded while still looking around. I checked out the bedrooms and saw the one that would be Mathias's room. It had a crib in there with a rocking chair. Along with a changing table. There was boxes and boxes of diapers and wipes in the closet. I was shocked. I went into the other room and had a huge king sized bed in there. A stand with a tv on top of it too. I went back out into the living room. "There's more furniture on the way in the next couple days. My parents and Bree helped me with it" he said. I nodded. "It's nice" I replied. "So what do you think?" He asked. "Okay" I answered smiling at him. He smiled back at me and kissed me.

Epilogue

"Mommy" Mathias said running up to me. I picked him up. "How was your day baby?" I asked. "Good. Auntie B let me have ice cream" he answered. I smiled at him. "What kind of ice cream?" I replied. "Chocolate ice cream with chocolate chunks" he responded. I laughed. Bree came into the room and smiled at us. "How was he?" I asked. "Really good. He was trying to teach me how to use the tv when I already know how and all he wanted to do was play with cars" she answered. I nodded. I put him down and he ran off to his room to play. I went into the kitchen and grabbed a water. "Jaxon is coming back tomorrow" she said. I nodded and didn't look at her. "It's been over a year since we broke up" I replied. "I know. But you know when he gets back from his trip he's gonna want to see Mathias" she responded. "And I won't stop him. That's his father" I said. She nodded. I took a drink. "Are you staying for dinner?" I asked. She nodded. I smiled. I got into the fridge and got somethings out.

"RAWR" Mathias yelled slamming his dinosaur down on the dinner table. "Thi thi" Bree said. I grabbed the dinosaur from him and replaced it with dinosaur chicken nuggets and Mac and cheese. He dug into the food. I sat down next to him and Bree. Then there was a knock on the door. I got up and went to see who it was. I opened the door. He was standing there with a bag over his shoulder. He smiled at me. I smiled back and opened the door. "Mathias you have a visitor" I said. He walked in. "Daddy" Mathias yelled running into his arms. Jaxon picked him up."Hey buddy" he said. "I've missed you" Mathias replied wrapping his arms around his neck. Bree came into the room. I closed the door. Jaxon put Mathias down and gave Bree a hug. "How's dad?" She asked. "He's good. He went to see mom" he answered. He looked at me. "How've you been?" He asked. "Fine. Mathias you have to go finish eating" I answered. He groaned and went back to the table. "Are you hungry?" I asked. "I could eat" Jaxon answered.

   "I'm heading out" Bree said. I nodded. She gave me a hug and went to go find Mathias. Jaxon and him disappeared after dinner into his room. She came out and smiled at me. "Mathias is really happy Jaxon is home" she said. I nodded. She grabbed her jacket and keys. She walked to the door and looked at me. "You know he hasn't been with anyone else. Maybe just maybe consider giving him another chance" she said then walked out. I rolled my eyes and shook my head. I sat down on the couch and turned on the tv. "Mathias" I yelled. He came running out with Jaxon behind him. "Wanna watch a movie before bedtime?" I asked. He nodded. He sat down by me. Jaxon sat down by him. I turned on a scooby doo movie and he was extremely happy. I smiled down at him. I looked at Jaxon. He was looking at me. I looked at the tv and watched the movie with them.

Mathias fell asleep half way through the movie. Jaxon picked him up and carried him to bed. I followed behind him. I tucked him in when Jaxon set him down on the bed. I kissed his forehead and turned out his light. We walked out of the room and into the hallway. Jaxon pushes me up against the wall. He leaned in close and kissed me. I pushed him away. "What's wrong?" He asked. "We broke up. A year ago" I answered. "Why was that again?" He replied. "Because you were an asshole to me. Treated me like shit near the end. Always getting angry towards me" I responded going under his arm and walking to the living room. He followed me. "I'm sorry. I was stressed all the time and I took my anger out on you" He said. "Saying sorry doesn't make up what you put me through" I replied. "Lena please. I miss you" he responded. I shook my head. I sat down on the couch and put nightmare on elm street on.

He stood in front of the tv. "Can we please talk about this?" He asked. I looked at his face. "I understand you were stressed at the time trying to find another job. You got another one. With your father again. All because you were stupid enough to quit because you thought that maybe just maybe it would be better at that one. But you. You were cruel to me. I cried myself to sleep many nights" I said. "I know. I was a dick and I've regretted it every damn day since. I was stupid. Because of me. We didn't have things that we should've. We struggled to make the bills. We struggled with getting Mathias everything he wanted and needed.

I knew it was my fault. But now I have a job. A good one. I've been trying to do better. Because I want my family back" he replied. I shook my head. "Maybe in time once I see that you are doing better" I responded. He shook his head. I got up and went to the kitchen to grab a drink. I grabbed a water and turned around. He pinned me there. He leaned down and kissed me again. He pulled the water from my hand and tossed it behind him. I shook my head and he smiled. I glared at him. He kissed me again and again. I gave up fighting him and kissed him back. I wrapped my arms around his neck and he lifted me up on the counter. He tugged at my shirt. I broke the kiss and looked towards the hallway while he started kissing my neck. "Bedroom" I said. He nodded and pulled me closer to him. I wrapped my legs around his waist and he carried me back to the bedroom.

"That so was not okay" I said laying on my side looking at him. "I want my family back" he replied. "I know. And I said maybe with some time" I responded. "I didn't want to wait" he said. "Jaxon I missed you. I really did. I don't think I've even stopped loving you for a second since it happened but I don't want what happened to happen again. I don't want to be treated like that" I replied. "Babe. After I lost my job and you I was nothing. I got my old job back and now all I want is you guys back. Please. Give me another chance" he responded. I took a deep breath. "Okay" I said. He gave me the biggest smile and kissed me.